W9-BFP-739

OTHER YEARLING BOOKS YOU WILL ENJOY:

YEARLING BOOKS are designed especially to entertain and en-lighten young people. Charles F. Reasoner, Professor Emeritus of Children's Literature and Reading, New York University, is consultant to this series.

For a complete listing of all Yearling titles,
write to Dell Publishing Co., Inc.,
Promotion Department, P.O. Box 3000,
Pine Brook, N.J. 07058.

THE WORLD'S GREATEST EXPERT ON ABSOLUTELY EVERYTHING... IS CRYING

by Barbara Bottner

A YEARLING BOOK

Published by
Dell Publishing Co., Inc.
1 Dag Hammarskjold Plaza
New York, New York 10017

Yearling ® TM 913705, Dell Publishing Co., Inc.

ISBN: 0-440-49739-6

Reprinted by arrangement with Harper & Row, Publishers, Inc.

Printed in the United States of America

May 1986

10 9 8 7 6 5 4 3 2 1

CW

for my mother

THE WORLD'S GREATEST EXPERT ON ABSOLUTELY EVERYTHING... IS CRYING

1

Tucker T. Cobbwebber marched up to Jesse's front door holding a giant tiger lily.

"Here," he said as he shoved it in her face.

"Thanks! Where did you get it? Did you pick it? Where?"

"You ask too many questions, Jesse Langston." Then Tucker grinned and tore off down the front lawn. A piece of paper gently floated down from his jeans pocket. Jesse ran outside and scooped it up.

GIOVANNI'S FLOWER SHOP
Tiger Lily, $1.00

Jesse's eyes were open so wide, they looked like brown copper pennies. Her freckled cheeks were puffed up in a big smile.

"Mom!" Holding the lily like a torch, Jesse tore inside and galloped past the kitchen into the living

1

room, where Mrs. Langston was reading the La Verne *Tribune*.

Jesse's mother put down her paper. "That's quite a flower."

"Tucker gave it to her," yelled the Hooter, Jesse's brother. He was stationed at the refrigerator door and peering into the living room like a junior spy. Her brother's real name was Gregory, but Jesse called him the Hooter because when he was a baby he hooted when he was hungry—which was almost always. *That* hadn't changed. In fact right now he was munching on a cucumber.

"Mmmmm," said Mrs. Langston, studying the lily, "I guess that makes Tucker your first official boyfriend."

"Mother!" Jesse yelled. "Don't *say* those things."

"He's Jesse's boyfriend? Because he gave her a flower?" asked the Hooter from the kitchen.

"Gregory, what *are* you doing in there?" Mrs. Langston asked.

The Hooter was looking inside the refrigerator the way some people look at television: all concentration, but in another world, far away from this one.

"I'm looking for high-energy food," he said.

"Why?" asked Jesse.

"Because this is going to be a crisis period."

"Hooter, where do you get these *words*?" asked Jesse. "You're only seven and a half."

"But I know a crisis period when I see one. Mom called Tucker your first official boyfriend. At least you have good taste," he mumbled, stuffing a handful of raisins into his mouth. "Tucker is cool."

Jesse took her flower and found a tall, thin vase, filled it with water, and snipped off the bottom of the stem as she had seen her mother do. Then she sniffed the flower.

"Tiger lilies don't smell," said the Hooter.

"They just *look* gorgeous," said Jesse. "And they last for a whole week."

"We'll see if Tucker lasts as long," said the Hooter.

"He will. He's in my class for the rest of the year."

Jesse took her flower into the living room and searched for the perfect spot for it. She wanted a place where anyone who came into the room would be sure to see it instantly. Jesse finally put it right on her dad's desk. She especially wanted to see the look on *his* face when he saw her flower. Then she walked over to her mom and leaned on the back of her chair.

"Hooter said Tucker will like me only for as

3

long as the tiger lily is alive," Jesse said in a quiet voice.

Mrs. Langston turned around. "Hooter is just being a tease. You have to trust your feelings. And Tucker's too."

"But sometimes I do feel strange when Tucker and I are in school," whispered Jesse, making sure the Hooter couldn't hear. "I like it better when he and I are just alone."

"Well, you have to believe that Tucker likes you even when he's busy with other people," said Mrs. Langston.

"I would like to," said Jesse. "But I get nervous."

The Hooter was suddenly leaning against the living room wall. "You can't *own* people, Jesse," he said. "Especially not Tucker. He's like me. Independent."

"I don't want to *own* anyone!" Jesse shouted.

Just then Mr. Langston walked through the front door, carrying a briefcase in one hand and his jogging sneakers in the other. He was tall and lanky even though he loved to eat. Just like the Hooter.

"Hi, honey. Hi, kids." He plopped his briefcase down in a chair, kissed everyone hello, and then moved Jesse's vase to the fireplace.

"Bad move," warned the Hooter. "A certain person is going to be insulted."

4

"Dad," said Jesse, before the Hooter could really embarrass her, "*I* put that flower on your desk. It was given to me . . ." Jesse waited for her dad to ask her who had given it to her, but he didn't, so Jesse had to finish: ". . . by Tucker!!"

Jesse waited for her dad to break out in a big smile and to see crinkly laugh lines form around his eyes. Instead he just asked, "Who's Tucker?"

"You're supposed to *know* Tucker," said the Hooter. "He's her new, first, and only boyfriend. She's waiting for you to be amazed."

"Hooter! He is *not* supposed to be amazed," said Jesse. "Anyway, it's only a stupid flower, and it's leaning the wrong way."

"OK, so who's Tucker, Jess?" Now Mr. Langston smiled as he took off his tweed jacket. "I've never heard his name before, have I?"

"Yes. Lots of times," said Jesse. "He's building the solar-powered doghouse, remember? And I'm helping him."

"Oh," said Mr. Langston. "The solar-powered doghouse inventor. I guess you did mention him."

"It doesn't really matter. He's just a boy, that's all."

"It is *not* all," said the Hooter. "Mother says he's her first boyfriend, and Jesse's all stewed up, aren't you?"

"Who asked *you*?" Jesse grabbed her jacket.

5

"I'm leaving," she said, glaring at her younger brother.

"I don't think love is making you a more patient person," said Mrs. Langston, managing somehow to look calm and happy. "Jesse, I want you home in half an hour, OK? Is Rosey coming over?"

"Yes!" Jesse slammed the screen door and ran down the block to Tucker's house. The light in the Cobbwebber basement was on, and from the street Jesse could make out a silhouette of Tucker peering into a box. He must be concentrating hard, because Pfeiffer, his dog, was barking and licking his foot, but Tucker wasn't even moving.

2

"Hi, Pfeiffer. Hi, Tucker," called Jesse as she bounded down the stairs.

Tucker didn't even glance up at her with his frog-green eyes. "Grab this tape" was all he said. Jesse didn't mind. When she was with Tucker, she always felt like she was around an important doctor about to perform brain surgery.

Tucker was working on his invention for "We Are Wonderful Day," which was coming up at the end of the month. Everyone in Mrs. Chakowski's fifth-grade class had to come in with a "wonderful" project. Jesse thought Tucker's project was the most wonderful, and she was proud to help him.

"It's got the solar panels already!" Jesse said.

Tucker peeked up at her and smiled. His ruddy cheeks puffed out under his glasses like two giant blowfish, and his sandy blond hair made him look slightly aglow. Suddenly there was the Hula-Hoop of silly excitement that Jesse always felt around Tucker. She would help him build a solar-powered kangaroo hut, if he asked.

Tucker took environmental issues very seriously. He was upset that Congress wasn't voting to preserve our coastlines, our forests, or the air we breathe. He'd demonstrated at a nuclear waste site two times. Once he fasted for a whole day to take a stand against strip mining. The more Jesse talked to Tucker, the more she realized that everyone had to do something to help the planet survive.

Sometimes Tucker seemed already a grown-up. He went to school, played softball, and did his homework like everyone else; but he also loved to read about people who'd made an impact on the world, watched hours of public T.V., and always had wonderful stories to tell about dolphins or family customs in China. Jesse loved listening to him, because he made all of life seem interesting. There was no one in the whole world like Tucker.

"You picked a great time to come over," said Tucker. "I'm having trouble with this duct. Can you hold the pipe for a minute? I want to check the irrigation system."

Jesse took hold of the metal pipe and held it so Tucker could solder it.

"Thanks for the flower. I put it in a vase," she said as she watched Tucker fiddle with some solder. Then she felt stupid. Where *else* would you put a flower?

"You're very welcome."

Jesse tried hard to keep the pipe steady. Then Tucker turned off the soldering iron and stood up. "I wonder if Pfeiffer will appreciate his house," he said. Pfeiffer was busy wagging his tail and begging for dinner.

"When is the lettering and the diagram going to be finished, Jesse?"

"I'll be finished with it in a few days."

"That would be great. Mankind . . . well, at least dogkind . . . is waiting. I've got to finish soldering this before seven thirty. House rules. Mom has a fit when I work too long. But she said if you came over I could ask you to stay for dinner. Want to?"

"Thanks, but I can't. Rosey's coming over. I'll see you at school tomorrow."

As she ran up the stairs to hurry home, Jesse thought burning metal smelled about as fine as anything could smell. Except possibly her mother's roast chicken.

3

"I suppose you were visiting the local genius again."
Rosey Roth was huddled in a green chair at the
foot of Jesse's bed, a chess book opened on her
lap.

"How did you know? Did the Hooter tell you?"

"I don't need the Hooter," said Rosey. "You
have that semihypnotized look you get. Like you've
been off in another galaxy and only half returned.
So how's Einstein doing?"

"Fine. I'm sorry I'm late, Rosey. I almost forgot
you were coming over."

"You forgot we were doing our homework together?"

"Well, I'm glad you're here," said Jesse. She
cleared a spot for her friend on her bed. Rosey
never worked at a desk. She claimed her best
thoughts wouldn't come to her if she was sitting
in a chair.

"That's more like it." Rosey fell down on Jesse's bed like a meteor falling from space: sudden and heavy.

Jesse stretched out on the pink Oriental carpet. It made her feel like she was visiting China. She was going to work on Tucker's lettering.

"What are you doing, Rosey?" Jesse asked.

"My book report. How do you spell Machiavelli?"

Jesse spelled it slowly. Machiavelli was Rosey's new hero; she had been reading about him for weeks. He had written a book called *The Prince* that taught you how to make people do exactly what you wanted them to do. Rosey was the class strategy expert, Room 203's own modern Machiavelli. But Rosey was different from him, because Rosey wouldn't do anything that wasn't honest. "I'd rather lose than lie," Rosey had once said.

But mostly Rosey had very good ideas and was able to get what she wanted, without lying. During the first week of school she'd gotten rid of Mrs. Crikland, the mean lunchroom manager, by drawing up a petition. Whenever Rosey needed to come up with a scheme, she'd gaze into the distance. Her blue-green eyes would turn into frozen marbles and then, Zap! She'd find a solution. That's why Rosey was class president of Room

203, the first person to be elected two years in a row.

Rosey was Jesse's best friend and they almost always got along—as long as Jesse didn't mention boys in general, or Tucker in particular. But not mentioning Tucker to Rosey was becoming harder and harder lately.

Jesse grabbed a library book about solar energy from her desk. "Did you know that solar heat is seventeen percent more effective than gas or electricity?" she asked Rosey. "It's the energy of the future."

"Nice," said Rosey, biting her pencil and looking off into space.

"Do you know what else? Tucker predicts that in the twenty-fourth century solar energy will be the number-one fuel."

"No kidding?" Rosey readjusted her position, and Jesse heard paper tearing. She looked up to see Rosey's book report in two pieces. Rosey made a face.

"You know what?" Rosey got up from the bed to get another piece of paper. "You sound like a Tucker clone." She tore a page out of her loose leaf binder. "Oh no! I tore out the wrong piece of paper. That was my *last* book report, and now I need to put reinforcements on it." Rosey went to look in Jesse's desk.

"Tucker says clones are the new thing." Jesse followed Rosey.

"Jesse, fine! If you want to be a boy-crazy clone, fine, fine, fine! But we're in the twentieth century. Females have a lot to offer. And we have to start now! That means each of us has to live up to her own potential. Do you read me?"

"I read you." Jesse found the box of sticky round circles Rosey was searching for and handed them to her friend. Then she went back to her spot on the floor to draw.

"But Rosey, suddenly I'm doing better than I ever did in science. I'm usually terrible. And you know it!"

Rosey was at the desk pasting on reinforcements. The tiny little circles were beginning to stick to her arm.

"You're improving for all the wrong reasons, Jesse." Rosey was making a mess. All the sticky circles were getting caught under her fingernails, and on her sleeves. "Personally, unless you're just getting lazy, I think you're wasting your talent working with Tucker. You should do your own project. After all, you do draw the best of anyone in the class."

Rosey was grimacing now. As she licked the first reinforcement and put it down, it went on her paper wrong. When she tried to lift it up, she tore the paper.

"These little circles are driving me crazy!" yelled Rosey. "Anyway, Jesse, I think *you* think you want to learn about science; but what you really want to learn about is boys. I'll be happy when you snap out of this." And with that Rosey managed to rip her entire page.

"This is disgusting," she said. "Talking about boys is making me into a nervous wreck."

"Let me help you."

"No thanks. I'm all gooey. I give up. I'm going home."

"You're not staying for dinner? It's roast chicken."

"No, I have to take a bath now." Rosey stood up, gathered her books under her less sticky arm, and headed toward the door. "Thanks for studying with me," she said. "It was unforgettable."

"Rosey! I can't help what's happening."

"I know," said Rosey. "That's the sad part. Well, you're still the nicest person around and my best friend." Then she was gone, making heavy clumping sounds down the stairway.

" 'Bye!" Jesse shouted.

Jesse went over to her mirror and brushed her hair for dinner. Last night she'd asked her mother to set her hair after her shampoo. Mrs. Langston was overjoyed. She said it was about time she had a daughter who didn't want to look like a wild woman from goodness-knew-where.

"Borneo?" the Hooter had asked.

"I have to admit," said Mrs. Langston just before dinner, "at least if love isn't making you sweeter, it's making you neater."

"Don't use that *word!*" Jesse shrieked.

"Which word?" asked the Hooter. "Sweeter, or neater?"

"*Neither!*"

"Love?" asked the Hooter. "Well, I'm for love. You aren't eating as many desserts these days, and I get all the extras."

"How boring it must be to be trapped inside a one-track mind forever."

"At least I still *have* a mind."

"Let's just see about that." Jesse grabbed the Hooter's vocabulary list from the table. Hooter had a larger vocabulary than anyone in his grade.

"Extricate," she challenged.

"Get free of," said the Hooter, munching an olive.

"Facilitate."

"Make easy to perform."

"Gruesome."

16

"Your preoccupation with Tucker."

"You're bluffing."

"Gruesome," Hooter repeated, biting a carrot stick. "Inspiring shock or repulsion."

"OK, you're off the hook," Jesse told her brother.

"That makes one of us," said the Hooter. "Meanwhile, do I get your piece of apple pie tonight, huh, Jesse?"

4

The next day Jesse walked Rosey home from school. Rosey's neighborhood was older than Jesse's. The houses were larger, with grand front porches, and the trees were hundreds of years old, and very tall. La Verne was one of the oldest towns in Connecticut. People said it was hardly on the map, and they wanted to keep it that way. Small, quiet, and friendly.

The girls walked briskly through the front yard. The orange and brown leaves were piled so thick, you couldn't walk through them without making a racket.

Inside Rosey's kitchen they dropped their books on the oak table. Rosey's mother made them hot chocolate.

"A new girl just moved in across the street," said Mrs. Roth. "She's going to be in your class, so I invited her over. I thought she should meet two of the nicest girls first."

"Us? We're not so nice," said Rosey.

"Well, Jesse's nice, and you're nice enough," laughed Mrs. Roth. "Anyway, her name is Katherine Ann Millicent Franklin."

"Why does she have so many names?" asked Rosey, her mouth covered with chocolate.

"Such fancy names, too," said Jesse. "Not like Jesse Langston, or Rosey Roth, which are about as interesting as a rock in La Verne Park."

"Speaking of park," said Mrs. Roth, "the leaves are parked on our lawn, waiting. So are the rakes."

When they finished their hot chocolate, the girls popped up from the table and went outside. They divided the lawn into territories.

"You be the North," said Rosey, "and I'll be the South. You can be General U. S. Grant and I'll be Robert E. Lee. OK?"

"Well, that means I'll win," said Jesse.

"But I'll be more colorful," said Rosey.

The North was slightly more raked than the South when a girl dressed in a pale yellow blouse came drifting into the yard. Long silky hair, with waves like a beautiful blond ocean, tumbled down her shoulders. As she came closer, Jesse noticed that she had two different-colored eyes. When you looked at them, you couldn't make up your mind which was more gorgeous: her gorgeous blue eye, or her gorgeous brown one.

"Hello. I'm Katherine Ann."

"Hi. This is General Grant, and I'm Robert E. Lee," said Rosey.

"She means I'm Jesse and she's Rosey. Did you just move in?"

"Yes."

"Where from?"

"From China."

"*China?*" said Jesse and Rosey together.

"Before that it was Sydney."

"Australia? Did you actually see kangaroos there?" asked Jesse.

Katherine Ann laughed. "Of course, but not in the city. We lived in England before we moved to Australia. You name it, we've been there."

"Wow!" said Rosey.

"Well, my father does important work with the government." Katherine Ann sat down in a pile of leaves and looked around. "In China there'd be sixteen people cleaning this yard, and they'd all be singing. Then they'd do everyone else's yard. Everyone works together."

Rosey and Jesse were almost speechless. This girl had lived in China!

"La Verne will be boring after all those other places you've been to," Jesse finally said. "It's only got one movie house, three restaurants, a tiny library, and one video arcade."

"Well, for some reason my father suddenly decided he wanted me to have a normal American childhood. We've never lived in any one place longer than a year. But I have a lot of interests, so I can be happy anywhere. Even La Verne, I guess."

Rosey looked at Jesse. They both knew they were dealing with an impressive person such as they had never met before.

"What *are* your interests?" Jesse asked, still dumbfounded.

Katherine Ann laughed. "We have a kiln, and I make pottery. I learned that in Africa. I collect rocks, do gymnastics, and cook breads from around the world. Oh, and I like to read poetry."

"Does that cover it?" asked Rosey. On her face was a rare look of amazement.

"More or less. Except for my secret thing, which, naturally, I can't talk about."

"A secret thing too? Oh, well, we don't do anything as exciting," said Rosey. "But I play chess, and I'm pretty good."

"She's very good," said Jesse. "Do you play?"

"Only when I don't have something more challenging to do."

"I draw," said Jesse. "It's my favorite thing to do."

"And she's good," said Rosey. "She'd be even better if she wasn't boy crazy."

"Rosey's just scared of boys," Jesse explained.

Both girls looked at Katherine Ann. Where did she stand on the boy topic?

Katherine Ann flicked her hair out of her eyes and looked up to the sky. "Boys are so insignificant, when you have a larger perspective," she announced.

Rosey nodded strongly in agreement, even though neither she nor Jesse was quite sure what Katherine Ann meant.

"I guess I should be getting back to help Mother unpack the bronze Buddha. We have our Indian rugs to put down, and the musical instruments to hang up. Mother will want me to help her arrange things. She says I have a good eye for negative space. Have fun with the leaves."

Then Katherine Ann floated away. Somehow, when she stepped on the leaves, they didn't crackle. Well, they crackled a little, but that was all. Someone as delicate as Katherine Ann didn't bother leaves the way Jesse and Rosey did.

"Wow!" said Rosey. "She's something!"

"I'll say. And beautiful."

"Probably rich too. Do you think she'll want to be friends with us? We're so regular."

"Everyone in La Verne is regular, compared to her," said Jesse. "Even Margaret Prince has only

been to Bridgeport twice. And New York City once."

"She'll probably like Margaret."

"And Margaret is going to fall at her feet."

"Come on," said Jesse. "I'm U. S. Grant, and the North is almost finished." Jesse picked up her rake and cleared under an old oak tree. But it was hard not to talk about this exotic new girl.

"Did you notice if her ears were pierced?" Jesse wanted to know.

"No, but did you see her two different-colored eyes? Weren't they incredible?"

"I bet only one person in a million has eyes like that."

"What do you think her secret thing is?" Rosey asked.

"I can't imagine."

"I wonder if we'll ever find out."

"I doubt it. What do you think she'll do for 'We Are Wonderful Day'?"

"It beats me." Rosey stopped raking. "I bet her father is a spy. Maybe we'll have counterspies sneaking all over La Verne. Wouldn't that be neat?"

"Well, Katherine Ann's certainly not a spy. Didn't you notice that she didn't even bother to ask us one thing? Not even about school." Jesse chased after some leaves that had blown away.

"Maybe we're too uninteresting. Too dull to be

friends with Katherine Ann. What do you think, Jess?"

Jesse didn't answer. She was wondering something else. Something she couldn't wonder out loud. Something that made her feel like there was a big hole inside her, and it was ready to get bigger.

Jesse was wondering what Tucker would think of this beautiful creature.

5

The next morning when Mrs. Chakowski introduced Katherine Ann Millicent Franklin to the class, she sounded proud, as if anyone with four names must be some kind of a prize. Everyone looked at Katherine Ann in her pink puff-sleeved dress and her woven shawl.

"Where do you think the shawl comes from?" Jesse whispered to Rosey. "China?"

"England?"

"Africa?"

Jesse looked over at Tucker. He was doodling. That meant he was most likely figuring out something about the doghouse. Jesse hoped it meant he didn't have time to concentrate on this new girl, who even wore perfume.

When Jesse looked back, Mrs. Chakowski was opening up a small package. "We are so lucky! Katherine Ann brought us some Congolese bread.

She lived in the Congo, where she learned how to bake it. Katherine Ann wanted all of you to taste what Africans eat."

Katherine Ann passed around small pieces to everyone. Margaret Prince's hazel eyes looked like a pair of grasshoppers about to jump.

"It's delicious," said Margaret. "I've never tasted anything like it. Not even in New York City."

Jesse chomped on her piece. It *was* good. She smiled at Katherine Ann, who gave the faintest smile back.

"Weren't you afraid of the wild animals?" Jesse asked.

"Most of the time we lived in a city. Africa isn't all jungle."

"Of course not," said Jesse.

"I'm sure Katherine Ann will tell us all about the many places she's lived," Mrs. Chakowski said, "but while she's passing around the bread, I'd like someone in Room 203 to explain what 'We Are Wonderful Day' means to the students at La Verne Elementary."

Michael Peters' hand was in the air, but Margaret Prince's skinny arm was up first, waving around like a dangerous tree about to fall over in a thunderstorm.

"Margaret?"

Margaret stood up. She was the tallest girl in Room 203. Margaret glanced at Katherine Ann nervously and cleared her throat. " 'We Are Wonderful Day' was created by our teachers to celebrate what people love. Nothing is too small or unimportant to share. The point is to *love* what you share. Last year Eric showed his collection of letters exchanged with an Indian boy on a reservation in New Mexico. Jesse did an art project on Civil War uniforms. Susan brought in her family album and explained how her ancestors traveled from Israel to Spain, and eventually ended up in Passaic, New Jersey. Wonderful things like that."

"Thank you. Katherine Ann, do you understand?"

"Yes, Mrs. Chakowski." Katherine Ann was nearly done handing out the bread. "But I may have a small problem."

And I may have a big one, Jesse thought. It seemed to her that Tucker T. Cobbwebber had forgotten about his doodling and was staring at the new girl with more interest than if she were a brand-new solar generator.

"You see," said Katherine Ann, "I can't be sure what to share; my Special Glaze Pottery, my Baking, or my Gymnastic Skills. I can do things that have never been demonstrated in the Western World. I can do . . ."

Tucker's eyes grew wider and wider as he listened to the list of Katherine Ann's talents. Jesse was beginning to feel woozy, and the more Katherine Ann spoke, the weaker and stranger she felt.

"Half her words are in capital letters," Rosey whispered to Jesse.

"You do gymnastics?" Margaret Prince was beaming. "I studied karate. And I—"

"That's very nice," said Katherine Ann calmly. "I learned karate from an old master in the orient."

"Wow!" said Margaret Prince. She was so impressed she could not speak.

"Of course there's one other thing I do," said Katherine Ann.

"There is?" Margaret found her voice. "What is that?"

"I can't talk about it. It's top secret."

If Princess Leia had just waltzed into the room with Darth Vader on her arm, Jesse doubted anyone in Room 203 could have stared with bigger bug-out eyes. From where she sat, Jesse could see Margaret Prince drawing a great big K and a great big A on her paper, and going over it in darker and darker pencil lines. Margaret will probably etch those pencil lines right through the paper and into the desk, she thought.

"Very interesting, Katherine Ann," said Mrs. Chakowski. "Well, why don't you just chew on your decision for another day? OK, class. After lunch we have drawing. And first thing tomorrow morning I will ask our class president, Rosey, to make a final list of what everyone is going to do. You have only until the end of the month to prepare for 'We Are Wonderful Day.' "

Then the bell rang.

In the cafeteria everyone crowded around the new girl. Everyone, including Tucker T. Cobbwebber.

Jesse wished she could do something to get his attention. Instead she just sat looking at her plate. She couldn't find her appetite. What if Tucker liked Katherine Ann better than he liked her?

Rosey, on the other hand, was putting away macaroni like a starving Italian child.

"I'm going to play myself at chess," Rosey said between forkfuls. "Nobody else plays chess, so it's up to me to show people what a great game it is. And you're still helping Tucker, I suppose?"

"After this morning I'm not so sure," Jesse muttered. "Maybe I should do something more unusual. Like have a mock funeral."

"Now that would be upbeat. You could borrow the skeleton from the nurse's office," said Rosey, devouring the last bit of food on her plate. "I bet you'd make the front page of the *Tribune*."

30

Margaret Prince plopped down beside them. "Guess what! You won't believe this, but I got invited to her *house*! I'm going to help her find a good place to look for rocks. Isn't that *incredible*?"

"If you say so," said Rosey, eyeing Margaret sideways. "And what are you doing for 'We Are Wonderful Day,' Margaret?"

"I have to do something *fabulous* so Katherine Ann won't be *bored* out of her mind. I mean, she might just *die* of boredom in this teeny town. We all just have to try harder this year."

"Really?" said Rosey.

"Oh yes. Jerry Grinder was going to read from *Dr. Dolittle*, but he's changed his mind. Instead he's going to read from *Pudd'nhead Wilson*. Everyone's project is becoming so much more ambitious now. I can't decide if the class is ready for an explanation about computer warfare, which my dad wants me to do, or if I should talk about women's rights, which my mother wants me to do."

"Well, what do *you* want to do?" Rosey asked.

"Me?" Margaret closed her eyes and her face lit up. "I'd like to demonstrate some karate moves."

"Why don't you?" Jesse asked.

"My mom and dad hate karate."

"But Katherine Ann probably likes it," said Rosey.

"You're right! Then maybe I'll do it! Are you going to play yourself at chess *again*, Rosey Roth, like you did last year, and the year before?"

"Yes," said Rosey. "Why?"

"Well, I thought you might like to know that there is someone else who plays. It might be more interesting for the rest of us, if you had a partner."

"Someone in our class is good enough at chess to face me? Who? Katherine Ann?"

"There is just so much one ten-year-old can do," said Jesse under her breath.

"No, silly," said Margaret. "It's Harold Smert. The boy who came in at the end of last year. He lives on my block and plays chess with my brother— and beats him! Harold's terrific. I told him you needed a partner."

"What?" said Rosey. "What did you do?"

"I told him," Margaret said, slowly enough for Rosey to read her lips if she had to, "that you needed a partner." She stared at Rosey with her hazel eyes, then jumped out of her seat and was gone.

"You're in luck, Rosey," said Jesse.

"You mean bad luck. Didn't you hear? She wants me to play with a *boy*! I don't want to play chess with Harold Smert. I don't even want to *talk* to him."

Rosey snuck a glance across the cafeteria. Harold Smert was looking at Rosey and cracking his knuckles. Sitting next to him was Tucker, who was babbling something to Katherine Ann Millicent Franklin.

"I wish I could just crawl under the table," said Rosey.

"Me too," groaned Jesse. "Me too."

6

Mrs. Chakowski was the shortest teacher in La Verne Elementary. She looked like she never had enough to eat, and she always wore bright-blue eye shadow and pink lipstick. Jesse was sure her sandy hair was dyed. Now she was buzzing around like a dizzy fly, stopping at one desk, then another, handing out drawing paper. She had asked everyone to draw something that fascinated them. Jesse let lots of images come to her mind, but one kept coming back: the tiger lily sitting in the glass vase, its pointy tips catching the light from the window. Jesse wondered if she could capture her beautiful present from Tucker on a piece of paper. She licked her lips and began to draw.

"Pssst! What are you drawing?" Rosey wanted to know. Rosey was the worst artist in the class. She depended on Jesse for ideas, but they never came out very well.

Before Jesse could answer, Margaret Prince was standing at Jesse's side, tapping her foot.

"Look at what Jesse's drawing," she announced to the class, her eyes positively glistening with mischief.

"Margaret, I've only just gotten started."

But soon several people had left their desks and were crowded around Jesse, the class artist.

"Pretty good," Rosey said, watching each line Jesse drew with great admiration.

"But Katherine Ann's is better," Margaret called from another part of the room. "Hers is complicated!"

"Children, please go back to your seats," said Mrs. Chakowski, who was now busy grading papers.

No one listened. Instead, all the bodies shifted across the aisles and bent over Katherine Ann.

What could that girl be up to? wondered Jesse. Something with shadows, or perspective, or lots of tiny details? Maybe it was a scene from one of the places she'd lived in. Jesse wanted to peek, but instead she concentrated. She would forget the rest of the class.

She carefully drew the long stem of the tiger lily, and got it just right. Jesse took a deep breath, but suddenly Margaret rushed by and knocked over her colored pencils. Jesse had to stop what she was doing and chase them as they rolled across the floor.

"Sorry," said Margaret.

It would take double concentration to forget about Margaret, whose specialty in life seemed to be in trying to become the world's worst pest. Then Jesse heard humming. It was Katherine Ann! She was coloring in something, with her tiny wrist flickering back and forth like a little bee.

"Jesse, you always draw the same kinds of things." Margaret was by Jesse's side again. Her eyebrows arched up towards her Indian headband and her hazel eyes were fixed on Jesse's paper. "Katherine Ann's drawing looks like it came right out of a book, it's so detailed."

"*Please*, children," said Mrs. Chakowski, finally getting up from her desk. "This is *not* a contest."

There were times when Mrs. Chakowski might as well have been a tiny bird trying to convince a herd of elephants to change directions. This was one of those times. Then Jesse heard a new voice chime in.

"Katherine Ann is really amazing." It was a boy's voice. It sounded familiar. It belonged to Tucker T. Cobbwebber.

"Jesse is the best," said Rosey.

"She's good," agreed Michael Peters, "but face it, Katherine Ann is in a different league."

"Never," said Rosey. "Never, *ever*, ever!"

Jesse's eyeballs were getting bigger by the minute. She was dying to get a peek at the big deal on Katherine Ann's page.

"They are both good," Tucker announced.

Jesse couldn't wait to hear what he would say next.

"Jesse," he began, "Jesse creates a feeling of mood in her work."

Jesse thought that so far this sounded pretty good.

"But Katherine Ann," Tucker continued, "has an uncanny ability to draw things as they really are!"

"Enough," Mrs. Chakowski squeaked. "I'm sure *everyone* will draw something worthwhile, if you just get *busy*! Now please get back to your seats, children."

"Can I have two more pieces of paper?" came a new voice. It sounded more like a song than a question. "I want to make a triptych."

"A triptych?" said Mrs. Chakowski.

"That's right," said Katherine Ann. "A three-part drawing."

"What a total show-off!" whispered Rosey.

38

"I want to draw the roof, the interior, and the basement," Katherine Ann explained. "That's what the newspaper wrote about."

"Rosey!" Jesse hissed. "What is she drawing?"

Rosey shrugged.

Jesse rose out of her seat. Feeling like a tidal wave about to break, she sprang over to Katherine Ann's desk, ready, she told herself, for anything. Anything at all. But when she saw what she saw, Jesse knew her life would never be the same. Tucker T. Cobbwebber was a lost cause. She slunk back to her seat.

"What'dja see?" Rosey whispered.

"Look for yourself."

Rosey got up, peeked at Katherine Ann's masterpiece, then moaned. On top of Katherine Ann's drawing was printed: SOLAR-HEATED HOME IN THE NEAR FUTURE.

"The plot sickens," said Rosey.

Margaret was still pacing the room, her hands on her hips, looking like an angry crossing guard. "Come on, Roth. If you were being really honest, on the basis of pure technique, you'd have to admit that Katherine Ann draws better than Jesse. Wouldn't you *have* to admit that if you were going to be *honest*?"

Everyone looked over at Rosey. They knew no

matter what, Rosey always told the truth. Rosey got up and slowly walked over to study Katherine Ann's paper again. Then, very quietly, with her head bowed down low, she whispered, "Yes."

Jesse bolted into the girls' room. Rosey rushed in right after her.

"Sorry. I had to be honest," said Rosey.

"I know, I know," said Jesse. "I wish I was never born. Tucker is like a flea that's found the perfect poodle."

"Jesse, you are making a big deal over nothing. What do you expect? After all, Tucker is just a—" Rosey could barely say the word —"boy."

Boys! Maybe Rosey was right. As soon as Jesse got home from school, she would get that tiger lily and put it into the laundry room, where she wouldn't have to look at it no matter how long it lived. Which she certainly hoped wouldn't be very long at all!

7

The next day Jesse was wearing her favorite bright-red turtle neck sweater. She thought it made her look like a glaring red traffic light. Katherine Ann looked more like a delicate snowflake, dressed in a soft powder-blue pinafore. And she was wearing a strange belt with tassels, which probably came from a small village on the Nile.

"Now," said Mrs. Chakowski, her pad and pencil ready for action, "let's see what kind of events we can look forward to for 'We Are Wonderful Day.' Rosey, as class president, would you please take notes so you can make up the order on the program?"

Rosey got out her pen.

"OK," said Mrs. Chakowski. "Let's start with the first row. Elsbeth Lee?"

"I'm going to sing a song from *The Sound of Music*."

"Very nice. Michael Peters?"

"I'm studying acrobatics. I'll demonstrate some tumbling combinations."

"How exciting. Jerry Grinder?"

"I'm going to dramatize a chapter from *Pudd'n-head Wilson* by Mark Twain."

"Excellent. Susan Northral."

"I'm bringing in my hand loom."

"That should be interesting. Rosey Roth?"

"I'll demonstrate some key chess moves."

"Like last year? How nice."

Rosey looked at Harold Smert. He smiled at her. Then Rosey looked at Jesse and wrinkled her nose.

"Margaret Prince?"

Margaret stood up. "Well, I'm going to demonstrate a minicomputer, and show how it can play war games."

"Thank you. Tucker T. Cobbwebber?"

"I'll be bringing in my solar-powered doghouse and telling how I made it."

"How fascinating. Katherine Ann Millicent Franklin?"

Jesse took a deep breath. What would the international wonder child come up with?

But the next voice she heard was Margaret's. "I changed my mind. I want to do a speech on women's rights."

42

"That's fine. Rosey, please change Margaret's choice."

Rosey scribbled on her pad.

"Harold Smert?"

"I'm building a chessboard from poplar wood. It has a leather binding."

"That sounds impressive. Oh, sorry, Katherine Ann, I skipped right over you."

Jesse looked over at the powder-blue girl. If Katherine Ann were to announce she was flying a helium balloon to Russia, nobody would be very surprised.

"Well, I can't decide," said Katherine Ann. "I'm having trouble making a single choice."

Suddenly Tucker was on his feet. "I have an idea. Since Katherine Ann is into solar energy, maybe she'd like to work with Jesse and me." Tucker turned to Jesse now, his green eyes flashing through his glasses like carnival lights. "Solar energy needs all the help it can get. What do you think, Jesse?"

"Sure," said Jesse. "Sure." And she nodded her head up and down even though every muscle in her head wanted to shake it back and forth, No. She wished the floor would open and swallow her up—fast. Everyone knew *she* was Tucker's helper.

"Thank you," said Katherine Ann. "I think I really might enjoy that."

Maybe Rosey was right. Maybe the time had come for Jesse to find her own project for "We Are Wonderful Day." Something she could do that would use *her* special talents. But what could that be?

It was Jesse's turn next, so she'd have to come up with an instant idea.

"And Jesse," said Mrs. Chakowski, "I guess you'll be doing—"

But Margaret Prince had jumped out of her seat again.

"Please cross out the speech on women's rights and put back minicomputers, OK, Rosey?"

"All right, Margaret. Do you think this is your final choice?" asked Mrs. Chakowski.

"Yes. Definitely."

Meanwhile, Jesse's eyes had been searching the room for a clue as to what she could say. On the bulletin board was a map of Mexico. Mexico . . . That was an exciting country. And one the famous world traveler in the next row had never been to. What could Jesse do that was Mexican? Learn to play the castanets? She didn't even know what they looked like. Or sing a Mexican song? No, they were all in Spanish, and Jesse was terrible with foreign languages. There must be something Mexican. . . .

"Fine. Margaret, you may sit down, and stay down. Now, Jesse, you're doing solar power with Tucker and Katherine Ann, isn't that right?"

"Oh! Me? Uh—actually—I changed my mind. I'm going to dance the Mexican Hat Dance."

The Mexican Hat Dance! Had *she* really said that? Well, if she had, at least she'd said something. And it wasn't solar power. Maybe her mother would send her to Mexico, and she would never have to return.

"You children never cease to amaze me," clucked Mrs. Chakowski. "Did you hear that, Rosey? Please write it down."

Rosey gave Jesse a sly little puzzled look.

"Well, thank you, class, for all your inventive and ambitious ideas. I'm sure the next few weeks will be very exciting."

Exciting was hardly the word. Harrowing was more like it.

"Why did you change your mind, Jesse?" Tucker wanted to know after class. "I was just trying to be nice to Katherine Ann, and make the best doghouse possible."

"Well, Tucker, now you will. You're in the best

45

hands with the solar-powered blue bloods. Good luck," said Jesse. She tried to smile at him, but instead her face made a funny twisted grimace. Thank goodness Rosey grabbed her arm and pulled her in another direction.

"Now you're in trouble, Jesse. *Where* will you learn that dance?" Rosey asked as they walked home.

"I'll start in the library. Come with me, OK?"

"OK. Look, I hate to say this, but you don't have to worry about Tucker. He still likes you. Yuck! And you shouldn't have quit the doghouse."

"And you should play Harold Smert at chess."

"Fat chance."

"Why not?"

"Because he's a boy."

"Well, boys make up half the human race, Rosey."

"Don't remind me."

"But you're going to be reminded anyway. Tonight. Margaret gave him your phone number. He's going to call you later."

"I won't *be* there!" yelled Rosey. "Come on, let's walk faster."

"Is the library open tonight?" Jesse asked her mother when she got home.

"Have an assignment?"

"Sort of. I quit the doghouse. Now I have to learn to do the Mexican Hat Dance."

"You quit the doghouse? Interesting," said the Hooter. "Why? What will your boyfriend say?"

"He's not my boyfriend. Especially since now he has a new girlfriend, Katherine Ann."

"Lucky him!" Hooter put down his whole wheat doughnut and picked up the La Verne *Tribune*. "Look what I found in tonight's paper." The Hooter read:

"Local residents plan solar experiment. Dr. and Mrs. Timothy Franklin, new in this area, have announced their plan to replace 40% of their residential electrical and gas services. by installing a solar-heating operation. This will include a solar cooker and rooftop solar collector. Dr. Franklin, a renowned scientist, has done research in this country, as well as in England, China, and Australia. His wife, Penelope D'Arrignville Franklin, and his daughter, Katherine Ann Millicent Franklin, have contributed valuable suggestions."

"How wonderful," said Mrs. Langston, who was listening from the living room.

"Want to hear the rest?"

"Certainly, Gregory," said Jesse's mother.

47

"Definitely *not*!" said Jesse.

"Jess, did you know that Penelope was friends with my old roommate, Ellie?" Jesse's mother came inside to see the paper. "She looks so glamorous, doesn't she?"

"What's more amazing," said the Hooter, staring at the paper the way he usually stared at the refrigerator, "is how beautiful Katherine Ann is. I think I'm in love."

Jesse headed for the front door. "This is horrible. I'm taking a walk. And I may never come back. But when I'm gone, remember that I was fond of you both."

Then she tore down the street like a speeding bullet.

8

"Rosey!" Jesse was at the front door of her best friend's house. *"Rosey!"*

Rosey popped her head out her window.

"What are you doing, Jess?"

"I'm going to the library hour. Can you come?"

Rosey hesitated. "I'm supposed to play my dad at chess in exactly one hour."

"We'll be back by then. Besides, I need you. I have to learn the Mexican Hat Dance, and I can't do it alone."

"You may not even be able to do it if you're *not* alone." Rosey still hesitated. "I don't know."

"Has Harold called yet?" asked Jesse.

"Harold? I forgot!" Suddenly Rosey pulled her head back in the window, bounded down the stairs, and ran out the front door. "Anything for a friend," she said, buttoning her jacket.

"Jesse, are you sure you want to go through

with this?" asked Rosey on their way to the library.

"No."

"Maybe you should just tell Mrs. Chakowski you want to work on the doghouse after all. So what if Katherine Ann can draw? You don't have to always be the best, Jesse."

"You don't understand."

"I guess not."

"Well, I've decided it's better if you have just one big problem instead of a lot of tiny small ones, like Tucker and Katherine Ann, that you can't keep track of. And learning the Mexican Hat Dance will definitely be one big problem. Know what I mean?"

"I suppose," Rosey answered. "But playing chess—that's a lot of small problems, building toward one big one—how to win the game. I guess I have a detailed mind. I *like* the little problems. Maybe I have a lot of folds in my gray matter."

"I hope your folds will come in handy at the library," said Jesse. "Like deciphering the card catalogue. OK?"

What the card catalogue told Jesse and Rosey was that Mexico was in the 970's. Rosey went to look in the correct aisle, while Jesse continued to look under Folk Dances and Dancing. She met Rosey at the front desk.

50

"Well, you can learn a lot about Mexican history," said Rosey.

"Or Mexican cuisine," said Jesse. "Maybe I can learn to make enchiladas."

"Or the Yucatán. But I don't think you're going to be able to learn the Mexican Hat Dance from any of these books."

"I'll take them anyway," said Jesse. "You never know."

"Let's go," said Rosey. "My dad's probably waiting for our game. Come on, let's walk *fast*."

"What about Harold?" Jesse reminded Rosey.

"On the other hand, let's walk like molasses," said Rosey.

The next day on her way to school Jesse couldn't wait to find out if Harold had called Rosey. Usually before the bell rang, everyone lined up in the school yard. But today there was no line, because Rosey and Harold had set up a chessboard and everyone was crowded around them. Rosey and Harold were both leaning forward, eyes riveted to the board. Their noses almost touched.

"If she takes his queen, she'll be in good shape," said Margaret Prince. "She's already got most of his pieces."

Suddenly Harold made what looked like a very

tricky move. Rosey just stared straight ahead. It took her a long time to make a move. When she did, Harold sat back, smiled, and removed her knight.

"That's a big deal," someone said.

Rosey didn't even blink. She studied the board like it was the inside of a computer. Everyone was quiet. In fact, the school yard had never *been* so quiet. Finally Rosey picked up one of her chessmen. Harold Smert cracked his knuckles. Rosey shot him a look. He stopped. After she moved her piece, only two of Harold's men were left. Rosey broke out in a wide grin. But it disappeared suddenly as Harold leaned forward again, with even more concentration.

Harold sat looking at the board for what must have been ten minutes. Even though no one knew much about chess, everyone sensed that something important was going on. Two people started playing catch, lost the ball, found the ball, and played catch again, while Harold still sat and stared. Finally the first bell rang. No one budged. Rosey was almost sweating. You could see her hands turning white.

Then Mrs. Chakowski came over.

"You heard the bell, children."

Suddenly an astonishing thing happened.

Katherine Ann bent over, her long blond hair sliding down and hiding her face, and whispered something to Harold. His hand darted out and moved his piece diagonally; and when he was through, Harold yelled, "Checkmate!"

A gasp went out through the crowd. "Harold won! Harold beat Rosey!"

Everyone but Rosey was buzzing as they lined up for class. She stayed put, staring at the board, watching it like it might speak to her.

"Come on, Rosey, let's go," said Jesse.

Rosey didn't budge.

"Come on, Rosey. Look, without Katherine Ann Harold wouldn't have beaten you. You can have a rematch on 'We Are Wonderful Day.' You'll beat him and get even."

Rosey looked at her friend. Her blue-green eyes were like those of an evil witch who was about to cook her children. "I'll get that girl," she said. "Somewhere, sometime . . . I'll get her!"

"Don't get carried away, Rosey. Didn't you just tell me last night that you don't have to always be the best?"

"Yes. But at least you lost fairly, Jesse. That's one thing. But I didn't loose *fairly*, did I?" She glared at her friend.

"I guess not."

54

"Katherine Ann embarrassed me in front of the whole class. Now I *have* to play Harold again." Rosey's eyes were almost slits by now. "Katherine Ann is a menace," she said. "It's all becoming clear to me now. While you're learning your dance, I'm going to think what to do about this problem."

Jesse knew Rosey meant every word.

9

That night at dinner Jesse hardly said anything.

"What's the matter, Jess?" her mother asked.

"I have to learn to dance the Mexican Hat Dance. Fast. And I can't find it in any of my library books. I'm going to be embarrassed in front of the entire class."

"Mortified," said the Hooter.

"Well, there must be a way to learn it," said her father. "How about dancing school?"

"Sure. Maybe in Acapulco."

"Come on, Jesse. We have an excellent dancing school right here in La Verne. We may be small, but we're not that small."

"But they'll never know a *Mexican* dance."

"It's a place to start," said Mrs. Langston.

"Or commence," said the Hooter. "I have to see this."

———

When Jesse and her mother walked into the La Verne Dance Academy the next day, Lania Fania, the head instructor, swept over to them.

"Can we interest you in ballet, tap, modern, jazz, interpretive . . . ?"

"We're looking for something very special," said Jesse's mother.

"I'm sure you are. I'm going to be busy for a few minutes, so why don't you just step inside and watch our jazz class? It's a great workout."

Before they knew it, Jesse and her mother were sitting on a bench in a huge room with wooden floors and wall-to-wall mirrors. Music was piped into the room from two enormous loudspeakers, and lots of ladies were stretching, jumping, and bending over while a teacher told them what to do.

"This looks like fun," said Mrs. Langston. "You know, maybe I should enroll."

"Could *you* do *that*?"

"Do you think I couldn't? I used to dance in college."

Two ladies leaped by. One woman seemed to find the whole thing terribly easy. She was in red and wore a headband. Her legs kicked higher than anyone's, and her stretches were stretchier.

"She looks familiar to me," said Jesse's mother.

"Why don't you sign up, Mom?"

"I just might."

At the end of the class Jesse and her mother went up to the registration desk. Mrs. Langston signed up for a trial class.

"And for the young lady?" Lania Fania asked.

"The reason we came here," said Mrs. Langston, "is we need to find someone who will teach my daughter how to do the Mexican Hat Dance."

"The Mexican Hat Dance . . ." Lania Fania closed her eyes and rolled her head around like a pelican. Finally she opened her eyes, scooted under the counter, and ran toward the dressing room. "Be right back!" she called.

While Mrs. Langston finished filling out a form, Jesse wondered if there was a Mexican Hat Dancer hidden somewhere in the dressing room. Suddenly Lania Fania swept back out, with the lady in red on her arm.

"Miss Langston, you are very lucky! I'd like you to meet our one and only Spanish dancer, Penelope D'Arrignville Franklin!"

The name buzzed in Jesse's head. Oh no! Were the Franklins taking over the world? Suddenly her mother was talking to the red woman.

"Penelope D'Arrignville Franklin! I thought you looked familiar. Welcome to La Verne. I'm Liz Langston. We both know Ellie Cooper."

"What a pleasure," said Mrs. Franklin, sweating in her tights. She extended a thin arm covered with gold jewelry. Jesse felt like she was shaking hands with a glamorous scarecrow.

"You know how to do the Mexican Hat Dance?" asked Jesse.

"Certainly, dear. And if you work hard, I'm sure I could teach it to you. It's not easy. Of course, my daughter, Katherine Ann, learned it very quickly. But she has a natural feel for the dance."

Jesse's mother put her arm on Jesse's shoulder. "Penelope, it's lovely of you to offer," she said. "Jesse is very coordinated. How can we arrange lessons without taking up too much of your time?"

"Oh, I think a few afternoons each week should do it. How does that sound to you, Jesse?"

Jesse could only nod. She wished Rosey was there to think of a way out of this.

"Turn around—let me see the whole of you," Mrs. Franklin said.

Jesse turned around, and as she did she tried to give her mother secret messages with her eyes, like "I don't want to go through with this."

Mrs. Franklin examined Jesse so carefully, Jesse got the willies. She tried to meet her x-ray gaze, but the woman scared her.

"Oh, excuse me, Jesse. I know I was staring. I just wanted to see what your proportions were. I thought I might be able to furnish part of your costume."

"That's very kind of you. Monday afternoon then?" said Mrs. Langston.

"Fine. By the way, Jesse," said Penelope Franklin, "did you know you are attempting to learn one of the most famous dances of Mexico? You must dance it splendidly."

Was Mrs. Franklin planning to invite the Mexican ambassador? It was perfectly possible that he was a dear old friend of hers.

"I didn't know," squeaked Jesse, "but I'll do my best."

10

On Monday morning Jesse was trying to pay attention in science class. That way she wouldn't have to keep thinking about her dancing lesson later that afternoon with Mrs. Franklin.

Mrs. Chakowski was setting up a microscope. She had promised that everyone would have a chance to look at things as small as a single cell! The assignment had been to bring in something to put under the microscope.

Jesse had brought in peanut butter. She was ready to smear it on a slide whenever Mrs. Chakowski gave the signal. But now Mrs. Chakowski wanted to know what everyone had brought.

"Rabbit tail."

"Piece of bark."

"A leaf."

"A fingernail."

"My dead goldfish."

"A snake."

Mrs. Chakowski looked up. "A snake? Who said that?"

"I did," said Katherine Ann. "I didn't know you had a lesson planned, so I brought in my snake from Africa. It had to be today, because my mother's making me give him away. We're donating him to the zoo, because he is so rare."

"That certainly is special," said Mrs. Chakowski. "A rare snake from Africa!"

Everyone was staring at Katherine Ann now.

"I think we should wait for our microscope experience until next week," said Mrs. Chakowski. "We don't study snakes until next year, but in this instance there's no reason we can't get a little head start."

Rosey looked at Jesse and frowned. "I hate snakes. I don't care if they speak Chinese and do arithmetic. This stupid goldfish will smell disgusting by next week. I had to rescue it from my neighbor's trash."

"Maybe you can freeze it," suggested Jesse.

Rosey made an awful face. She wasn't the only disappointed person in Room 203.

"Why does Mrs. Chakowski always let Katherine Ann do what she wants?" Elsbeth Lee asked at lunch.

"I don't know," said Jerry Grinder.

"Don't you like snakes?" asked Michael Peters. "She was only trying to share."

"I'm getting a little tired of all her sharing," said Susan.

"Everyone is getting fed up with Katherine Ann," Rosey whispered to Jesse. "And it's only going to get worse."

Later that afternoon Room 203 watched as Jerry Grinder helped the gym teacher demonstrate some beginning somersaults. Jerry had just finished his first roll when Katherine Ann piped up.

"Your form isn't exactly right," she said.

Jerry suddenly looked like he might get sick.

"This is how I was taught," he stammered.

"You don't tuck in your head early enough," said Katherine Ann firmly.

"Katherine Ann," said Miss Rider, the gym teacher, "if you have another way, why don't you show us?"

Katherine Ann got on the mat. "You stretch your arms like this," she said.

Jerry Grinder's face was getting blotchy. "Exactly what I did," he sputtered.

"No, your arms were too straight. They can't take the ground fast enough like that," said Katherine Ann. "See?"

Over she went, and bounced back up like she expected T.V. cameras to be on her. "Can you tell the difference?"

"Not exactly," said Jerry. Now his voice sounded sad, and he walked to the end of the line. "But it really doesn't matter."

Jesse didn't like to see Jerry look so defeated, but she had other things on her mind.

"Psst! Rosey! What if she's like this when I have to learn the Hat Dance? It's going to be terrible."

"You might have to strangle her," said Rosey, "which would be doing the rest of us a great favor, if you ask me."

"I heard that," said Margaret Prince. "And if you ask *me*, even though she may overdo it sometimes, Katherine Ann just wants to give us the benefit of her rich experiences."

"If she's not careful, she's going to get some rich experiences she never bargained for," said Rosey. "She's getting on a lot of people's nerves."

"Well," said Margaret, puffing up her chest, "I guess you have to be a big enough person to be able to appreciate someone like Katherine Ann." Margaret walked back to her place in line.

"When Margaret's had enough," whispered Rosey, "then we'll know it's time to act."

11

After school Jesse walked up to the Franklins'
enormous carved-oak front door. It looked large
enough for an elephant to fit through. She rang
the bell.

"Jesse, I've been waiting for you. Take off your
coat, and we'll begin." Mrs. Franklin was wearing
makeup today, and her face was beautiful. But it
wasn't the kind of beauty that made you feel warm
or comfortable. It was another kind of beauty, one
that made you feel stubby, creased, and like you
needed to brush your hair, even if you already
had.

Jesse looked around. She had never been inside
such a large and fancy home. There were African
sculptures, Oriental tapestries, and a table full of
exotic musical instruments. Jesse's eyes raced to
take everything in.

"Oh dear, you really should have worn a long

skirt to get the feel of this dance," said Mrs. Franklin, who was wearing a big skirt and a shawl. "Oh well, you'll just have to pretend, I guess. Let's get started. As I'm sure you know, Jesse, this dance is derived from the bolero." Mrs. Franklin rolled the "r" and flashed her eyes. "The steps are of Spanish and Mexican origin. Some are imitative patterns, like the prance of a horse, or the courtship of doves. Some are telling ancient stories of love."

Jesse was beginning to wonder if Mrs. Franklin would ever stop talking and start showing her the steps.

"Naturally, you will have to *spring!*" continued Mrs. Franklin. Suddenly she sprang into the air like a large, graceful jack-in-the-box.

"You will also stamp!" Mrs. Franklin put her right foot forward and stamped the floor several times, first with the ball of her foot, then the heel. "Remember, always move your shoulders, and hold the skirt like this. This is a courtship dance. You must be coquettish. Ready?"

In her mind Jesse was renaming "We Are Wonderful Day" to "We Are Ridiculous Day."

"Yes."

Mrs. Franklin put the record on. The music was very gay, and suddenly she was off clicking her heels, stomping, twirling, shouting "Olé" and throwing her head back so her chin was in the air.

"Like this, Jesse! Do what I do!" She was almost singing.

Jesse plunged in. She stomped with her left foot, once, twice, but the third time it came down on something mushy.

"Oooh," said Mrs. Franklin, grabbing her foot.

"Sorry," said Jesse. "I didn't know you were there."

"Jesse, you must be free, but not careless!" Mrs. Franklin began to dance again, starting with a twirl.

Jesse decided to twirl too. She twirled full steam ahead, and turned, and turned. The next thing she knew, the entire room was spinning. She grabbed a chair, hoping it would stop. It didn't. So Jesse let go, still trying to balance herself, and walked straight into a wall.

"You aren't *dancing*, my dear!" Mrs. Franklin swept over and took Jesse's hands. "Like this. Prance, and cross, and turn. Look over the shoulder. Shout 'Olé!' "

The only thing Jesse wanted to shout was "Help!"

"I can't learn this fast," said Jesse, planting her feet firmly on the floor. There was no point in pretending.

"I don't blame you," said a voice behind her.

Jesse turned around to see Katherine Ann standing at the entrance to the living room. Her hands were on her hips.

"Mother, Jesse's never done this before." Katherine Ann almost sounded like she was scolding her mother.

"Katherine Ann, you're supposed to be out collecting local rocks."

"I'm tired of rocks." Katherine Ann plopped down in a chair.

"Well, find something else to do. I won't have you watching Jesse. You'll make her self-conscious."

Jesse agreed. She couldn't imagine trying to learn the dance with Katherine Ann there.

"Jesse looks a little dizzy," said Katherine Ann. "Mom, why don't we stop and have a snack?"

"OK. I guess we could take a little break."

Katherine Ann led the way, and Jesse and Mrs. Franklin followed down the hallway.

"At least you're getting to do what you want to do for 'We Are Wonderful Day,' " Katherine Ann said when they reached the sprawling old kitchen.

"I don't want to hear this," Mrs. Franklin warned. "What you would like to do, Katherine Ann, is simply out of the question."

Jesse would have loved to ask what that was,

but it didn't seem smart to get in the middle of Katherine Ann and her mother.

Mrs. Franklin poured milk and put some banana bread on a plate. Then Katherine Ann asked Jesse a question, the first question she'd ever heard Katherine Ann ask about another person. Still, she wished the girl hadn't bothered.

"So—how long have you been fascinated by Mexico?"

Jesse gulped down her milk. What could she say? Ever since the minute you joined Tucker's team?

"Oh," said Jesse, thinking fast, "I think Mexico is worth a whole lifetime of study." And then she took a bite of banana bread and pretended to chew it very carefully.

"Well, we don't have a lifetime to study this dance," said Mrs. Franklin. "So let's get back to it!"

"How'd D day go?" Rosey asked the next morning. "Get it? Dance day."

"Very clever. But Rosey, if you think Katherine Ann is trouble, you should meet her mother."

"You mean she's worse? How?"

"What are you two whispering about?" Margaret Prince stalked up. "You're always having secret meetings. Well, if you can stop for one minute, I'll tell you something absolutely exciting. Ready?" Margaret Prince could hardly catch her breath. "I have made a momentous decision. I'm going to do a karate demonstration. And you two helped me decide."

"Congratulations," said Rosey.

"Good luck," said Jesse.

Katherine Ann walked over and joined them.

"It's amazing, isn't it?" said Margaret proudly. "I'm doing karate for 'We Are Wonderful Day.' "

"How many lessons have you taken, Margaret?" asked Katherine Ann.

"About ten."

"Only ten?" said Katherine Ann. "You're a brave girl."

"I am?"

"Sure, I've taken dozens of lessons, and I wouldn't dare get up there."

"You wouldn't?"

"I'd hate to make a fool of myself."

"Oh. Of course."

Then Katherine Ann disappeared down the hallway.

"Well, Margaret, I think it's great you decided to give it a try," said Jesse.

"I *thought* I had decided," Margaret admitted. "But suddenly it seems stupid."

"It's just that girl, Margaret," Rosey said.

"She might be right. I could make a fool out of myself."

"Don't let her get you nervous," said Jesse.

"She's been getting to everybody," said Rosey. "Think about it." Rosey's eyes widened.

Margaret bowed her tall head down. "I hate to say this," said Margaret, "but now that you've reminded me, I realize that girl is driving everyone crazy."

"You bet she is." Rosey looked at Margaret as if she'd just gotten a bright idea. "And I think it's time for action."

12

"You have a plan already?" Jesse asked after Margaret had left school that afternoon.

"Not yet," Rosey said on their way home. "But I will. All I have to do is tell my brain to get to work on it."

"It's that easy? When will you tell your brain to get started?"

Rosey closed her eyes. "Now. *Shhhhh*. I have to concentrate." Jesse didn't say a word. Neither did Rosey. They walked all the way down the block.

"Can you make a plan where Katherine Ann learns to be nicer?"

"That's the *idea*, Jesse."

"How about a plan where she becomes ugly? Grows warts, and hairy arms?"

"I'm a strategist, not a magician." Rosey shut her eyes again, then opened them. "OK. It's in the works."

"When will we know?"

"Soon."

"Will you tell me first?"

Rosey looked at Jesse with her big eyes wide open. "Do dogs bark?" she asked.

"Do fish swim?"

"Do cats meow?"

"Do boys play chess?"

"Ugh!" said Rosey. "Did you have to bring *that* up?"

Jesse and Rosey had reached Rosey's block. They stood on the corner talking.

"Are you going to play Harold for 'We Are Wonderful Day'?"

"I was roped into it. I'll never forgive Margaret for being such a busybody. Boys are the worst."

"What do you mean by that?"

"They're dumb."

"How?" Jesse asked.

"They laugh at things that aren't funny."

"Does Harold do that?"

"Maybe not," said Rosey, "but most of them do. They act wild and immature."

"I never saw Harold act that way."

"Well, Harold *is* sort of quiet. But quiet is just as bad anyway. Besides, all they care about is sports."

"But Harold likes *chess*!"

"This is an unbelievably boring conversation, Jesse. Anyway, I've got to be quiet so my brain can work. I'll see you tomorrow." Rosey turned to walk home.

Jesse felt a little laugh simmering in her chest, but she made sure Rosey was far down the block before she let it boil into a giggle. She wondered if the day would ever come when Rosey would feel the way she did about boys. But on second thought, the way she felt right now was not something to wish on anyone.

When Jesse got home, she decided to do some more research on Mexico. She sat in her big comfortable chair and opened her library book. She read that a child in rural Mexico would sometimes be wrapped in its mother's *rebozo* while she worked in the fields. She learned that Mexico's most important crop is maize, and that some old dances were thought to make crops grow. Tlaloc, the Aztec rain god, had his very own dance. Jesse was wondering if she could ever put the right meaning into *her* dance when the Hooter popped into her room. He was grinning from ear to ear.

"You have an interloper," he said.

"A *what*?" But the Hooter was already scampering down the hallway. Hooter and his big words. Why did he always have to interrupt her?

Jesse put a bookmark in her Mexico book and went downstairs. Tucker T. Cobbwebber was pacing up and down her living-room floor.

"Hi, Jesse. How's the dance coming?"

Jesse tried to smooth her hair. "OK. I was just reading about Mexico."

"I guess you really love your new project," said Tucker.

Jesse didn't know what to say. "How's the doghouse coming?" she finally asked.

"Well, on Sunday Katherine Ann took me over to meet Mr. Franklin. You'll never guess what he did."

"What?" Jesse wished she could hear Katherine Ann's name without feeling that she wanted to sit down and never get up again.

"He took me to a solar research plant! Where they conduct studies on how to convert energy. He showed me all around. He sure is a big shot."

"Gee, that sounds exciting, Tucker." Jesse tried to be enthusiastic.

"It is! Hey, Jesse, I'd like to take another look at the lettering you started for the doghouse. If you don't mind."

So that's why Tucker had come to visit! She should have known.

76

"It was Katherine Ann's idea. She said we shouldn't let anything go to waste. Very ecological of her, isn't it?"

Tucker seemed so proud of his reasoning that Jesse wanted to sock him in his ecological face.

"Sure, Tucker. Right this way." Tucker followed Jesse upstairs to her desk. She handed him pages from a large art pad.

"Thanks." Then Tucker's face changed a little. He almost looked sad. "I wish you were still working on the doghouse, Jesse," he said. "But I can see that learning that dance is much more challenging for you. And it's something all your own. I don't blame you for switching."

As Tucker walked downstairs to the front door, Jesse wished she could tell him the real reason she had quit. But he would never understand. Never in a million years.

"You know, Jesse, Katherine Ann is a very hard worker," he said. "I think she wants to learn about solar power because that's what her dad is all about."

She wants to understand what *you're* all about, Tucker T. Cobbwebber, was what Jesse thought.

"Still, I'll tell you one thing," he continued. "She's not *you*!" And then Tucker was out the door.

What? What did he mean by *that*? Jesse stood there stunned.

The Hooter suddenly materialized in the living room. "Did he leave? I wanted to talk to him. Tucker always knows neat facts."

"Well, he and his neat facts are gone. And I don't think they'll be back."

"Too bad," said the Hooter. "Oh, Jesse, guess what?"

"What?"

"It's about your tiger lily."

"Spit it out, Hoot."

"It's kind of droopy and sick-looking. Didn't you keep the water fresh?"

"It doesn't matter anymore," said Jesse.

"Love is strange," muttered the Hooter. Then he went off to find a snack.

The next day at school Margaret was waiting for Rosey and Jesse when the bell rang for lunch. "Well, what did you come up with, Rosey? I hope it's not too extreme."

"I considered a lot of elaborate plans, Margaret. I gave it real thought. I even skipped T.V. last night so I could have a clear head. But I decided that in this case the best medicine is the old-fashioned cold shoulder."

"*That*'s your big plan?" Margaret's voice climbed up an octave. "I could have come up with something *that* simpleminded. *And* watched five sitcoms, plus the news."

"Margaret! We have to start small. If nobody talks to Katherine Ann for a day, I think that will change her style a lot. And it just so happens this technique was used by primitive tribes. Whenever someone committed a crime, the tribe would act like that person wasn't there. They looked right past them. They didn't hear them. See? They called it the Living Death."

"The Living Death," said Jesse. "It has a certain ring to it. What do you think, Margaret?"

"Maybe. But let me concentrate for a minute." Margaret turned her back to the girls. "Wait a minute!" She suddenly spun around. "Let's all become just like Katherine Ann. Only worse."

"You mean imitate her?" Jesse asked.

"Exactly. Give her a chance to see what she's really like. A taste of her own medicine."

"But how can we do that? We don't have her experiences—"

"Then we'll fake it. Pretend."

"Well, that might be effective," said Rosey. "But personally, I don't like lying. I wouldn't do it."

"It's not lying. It's exaggerating."

"Exaggerating is a form of lying," said Rosey.

"Well, then, let's do both!" said Margaret. "Everyone will have a choice of imitating her or the Living Death. I think between those two tactics, we have a chance of making some real improvement in Katherine Ann. Let's face it, Katherine Ann can really be pretty neat, when she's not being . . ."

". . . the world's greatest expert on absolutely everything!" said Rosey.

"Right. I'll pass the word around," said Margaret. "It's either the Living Death or . . . the Mirror Effect!" She shook Rosey's, then Jesse's, hand vigorously, and skipped off to begin her work.

13

"I can't believe it," Margaret Prince whispered to Rosey and Jesse at their lockers that afternoon after school. "Know what Katherine Ann did to Elsbeth Lee? She told her she used to sing the same song from *The Sound of Music* that Elsbeth is singing for 'We Are Wonderful Day'—in French! Elsbeth nearly had a heart attack. Then when she came up for air, Katherine Ann told her that *that* was when she was seven years old. Can you imagine? The girl is positively insensitive."

"So is Elsbeth in on the plan?" Rosey wanted to know.

"Of course. Everyone's in on it, except Tucker. Did I tell you that Katherine Ann actually suggested that Elsbeth might like to learn a verse from her in French?"

"What did Elsbeth say?" Jesse asked.

"You mean after she turned the deepest shade

of purple? She told Katherine Ann she thought she'd just stick to the English. But now Elsbeth says she may sing it in a higher key, way at the top of the soprano range."

"Elsbeth has a beautiful voice," said Jesse. "She doesn't have to worry."

"No, but *I* have to worry," said Margaret.

"And *I* have to worry," said Jesse.

"And *I* have to worry," said Rosey.

"Why Rosey? You always play chess," Margaret said.

"Not with *boys*, Margaret Prince! Not with Harold Smerts!"

"Oh, Rosey!" said Margaret. Then she closed her locker, gave a sort of salute, and was off.

"I'm glad she's on our side," said Rosey. "She's a little overzealous."

"Over what?"

"Overzealous. It means doing things gung ho. Like calling up Harold, when no one asked her to."

"Well, hello, Jesse!" Mrs. Franklin was moving some furniture, a big basket, and some plants out of the way in her living room to make space for an enormous Mexican hat. "Did you practice your steps, dear?"

"I tried."

"There's no such thing as trying. Either you did or you didn't. I'll put on the music and we can find out."

Mrs. Franklin put the record on the turntable while Jesse tried to remember the little heel-toe movements.

"Jesse, Jesse, Jesse! You can't just forget the rhythm, darling. Can you *hear* that beat? Ta tooom, ta tata toom . . ." Mrs. Franklin had arched her back and was ready to dance.

"Watch this." She clicked her heels and twirled, then leaped. She kept going faster and faster, moving in a frenzy. Jesse had to step back. Mrs. Franklin seemed to take up the whole room. Her head rolled from side to side, and Jesse noticed her eyes flickered closed. Mrs. Franklin had danced herself to another planet.

"Ta ta ta toom, ta toom, de da da doo, ta too." Mrs. Franklin leaped across the room, while Jesse shrank farther and farther back toward the wall. "Do as I do!" Jesse began to worry that Mrs. Franklin might knock over one of her expensive vases, or tumble over a chair. "You must *give* yourself to the dance," she said to Jesse, waving her arms.

Was Mrs. Franklin trying to exhaust herself?

Jesse didn't understand how she could give herself to the dance, when she didn't know how the steps *went* in the first place.

"Well, Jesse, that should help you visualize how it looks." Mrs. Franklin had stopped dancing, and was breathing hard.

"I guess."

"You guess? I didn't knock myself out for a guess. Now, are we ready to dance together? Head up, back arched, foot pointed, and a great big smile on your face. Let's go!"

The needle came down on the record just as the phone began to ring. "Darn it, that will be Mr. Franklin. Be right back!" Mrs. Franklin stopped the record and swooped off to another room as if there was a crowd cheering her.

Jesse stared at the big hat on the floor. It was hopeless. She felt tears coming to her eyes. She couldn't learn how to thread a needle from Mrs. Franklin, let alone a complicated dance. Even though the woman really seemed to be trying, it just wasn't working out.

What a mess!

"Hello." Jesse looked up and saw Katherine Ann standing in the doorway.

"Hello."

"You don't look so good," said Katherine Ann.

"It's that dance. I can't learn it."

"Do you want me to show you the opening sequence?" asked Katherine Ann. "Watch this." Katherine Ann arched her back, positioned her arms, and pointed her toes. "See, you point, you twist, you snap, bend, and point again. Try it."

Jesse positioned herself behind Katherine Ann. "Point, twist, snap, bend, point again. That wasn't so hard."

"I know. Do it again."

Jesse tried it again.

"Not bad. Now try tap, tap, tap, jump, skip, turn."

"Tap, tap, tap, jump, skip, turn."

"You did it fine, Jesse."

"I can't believe it. I can't believe I finally learned those steps. Thanks, Katherine Ann."

Katherine Ann smiled and then looked away. Suddenly she turned and said, "I never had any real girlfriends, Jesse. I think I would like some."

Jesse was stunned. But before she could think of anything to say, Mrs. Franklin came hurrying back through the doorway. "Katherine Ann, don't bother Jesse, please. You have plenty of other things to do."

"Right," said Katherine Ann, and she scooted out of the living room.

"Now, let's see you dance." Mrs. Franklin turned

the record on. Jesse did the steps the way Katherine Ann had taught her. How had she made it so much easier?

"Fine, Jesse, fine," said Mrs. Franklin. "I guess I'm not a failure at this after all. OK, are you watching?"

Jesse took a deep breath and glued her eyes on the whirling, spinning, leaping person in front of her.

The next day in the lunchroom everyone was wondering what the special of the day, moussaka, was. Nobody had ever heard of it before.

"Moussaka is made with eggplants and meat," Katherine Ann told Elsbeth Lee while they stood in line. Elsbeth looked around as if she heard a sound coming from the hallway, but she never answered Katherine Ann.

"My mother learned it from a Greek cook who worked for us in London," Katherine Ann continued. "I *love* Greek food, don't you, Elsbeth?"

Elsbeth pretended to look for a quarter in her purse.

"Don't *you* love Greek food, Margaret?"

Margaret Prince started to open her mouth, but she closed it quickly. Instead she opened her notebook and began searching for a book report.

Katherine Ann pushed her hair aside. She didn't

know what to think. "I guess nobody around here is really that interested in food," she finally said. "The thing is, cuisines from around the world are so interesting. Like the curry you can get in England. Ever try curry?" Katherine Ann asked Harold Smert, her voice sounding just a little bit tense.

"I'm allergic to eggplant," Harold said to the lady behind the lunch counter as he moved down the line away from Katherine Ann.

"I always said you were a fascinating boy, Harold," called Margaret. Then she buried her head back in her book report.

Katherine Ann began to shift uneasily from one foot to the other.

Jesse was standing a few people down from her and saw the predicament Katherine Ann was in. She prayed she could manage to fade into the line without being detected.

"I mean, doesn't anyone know Greek food?" Katherine Ann suddenly asked very loudly, looking at everyone. But no one would answer. Finally, Katherine Ann stepped out of line and began to walk up and down it like a monitor.

"Ever hear of lemon soup?" she almost shouted. "It's very good. And I especially enjoy spinach pie. Of course you can't beat feta cheese, which comes from a *goat*."

On the word "goat" Jesse thought Katherine Ann was going to shake someone, because no one would even look her way. Now Katherine Ann was heading directly for Jesse. Jesse panicked. When Katherine Ann was one person away from her, Jesse suddenly flung out her arm and swung around in a move she'd learned from the Hat Dance. Only this time there was a shelf of Jell-o in the way. Dishes of Jell-o went flying down the cafeteria line and crashed to the floor.

Jesse and everyone else, grateful for the distraction, scampered to clean up the mess while Katherine Ann stood in front of them dumbfounded.

But it also seemed to Jesse that the exotic Katherine Ann was slowly figuring out that she was being snubbed by a bunch of small-town nobodies.

Amazing.

That afternoon, in Room 203, Mrs. Chakowski was discussing the day's geography assignment— the rivers of the United States. She asked people to name their favorite rivers and tell everyone why. Katherine Ann was the first to get called on.

"The Mississippi River," said Katherine Ann. "My father was born on the Mississippi. His family is distantly related to Mark Twain's. My grandfather was a logger, and my dad was the first person from his town ever to go to college."

"Fascinating," interupted Michael Peters. "But not as fascinating as the Colorado River. At least to me. In fact, I have brought in an actual *rock* from that esteemed waterway. My family and I were there interviewing various fish for my father's fish market. I don't know if you saw our pictures in *National Geographic* last month. Oh, and here is the original rock I was talking about."

Michael handed around a cruddy, gray, everyday rock. People began to snicker.

"I'm not familiar with the Colorado River," said Susan, "but *our* family was one of the very first to settle on the Hudson River. The Hudson Northrals—I'm sure you've heard of us."

Rosey was chewing on her ponytail so she wouldn't laugh when Jesse looked at her. Margaret had her head buried in her hands.

"We are the same Northrals as those of the Northral Timber Company, which just about *built* colonial America. Here is an authentic piece of wood from that period of American history."

Susan proceeded to pass around a piece of wood that looked as if it came off her fence.

Mrs. Chakowski looked slightly bewildered, but Katherine Ann didn't. She was sitting in her seat, mouth shut as tightly as a bank safe. Tucker was scribbling in his notebook. Jesse wondered if he knew what was going on.

"*Pssst*," Margaret whispered to Jesse. "I think the Mirror Effect is going pretty good. Don't you?"

Jesse nodded. But for some reason this whole enterprise wasn't making her feel better.

"Personally, I like the Wisconsin River," said Margaret. "I was up in the northern part of that state examining the glaciated terrain. We Princes, of course, are the same Princes who scaled Everest in 'forty-eight. Anyway, I brought in something that was found in the Wisconsin River bed."

Margaret passed around a shoe box, which everyone peeked into. When Jesse's turn came, she started to giggle. Inside was an Old Milwaukee beer can.

"I don't know *what* is going on here," said Mrs. Chakowski, "but I can see you are *not* taking this lesson seriously. I *don't* find it amusing."

Katherine Ann stood up. "They're not making fun of you, Mrs. Chakowski. It's *me* they're imitating."

She turned and faced the whole class, but no one would look at her.

Suddenly the Mirror Effect and the Living Death seemed like terrible ideas to Jesse.

"Isn't it?" asked Katherine Ann. But nobody

answered her. "Well, I don't care. You're all just small-town nothings. You don't mean anything to me. I don't care whether you like me or not."

"That's a lie." Jesse was suddenly speaking. "You do care and you know it. You told me yourself. Remember?"

"Well, you're wrong. So just keep quiet, Jesse, OK?"

"I can't believe you betrayed the Living Death, Jesse," hissed Margaret. "How could you?"

Rosey buried her head in her hands and moaned.

"*What* are you mumbling about, Margaret? What is the Living Breath?" asked Mrs. Chakowski. "Someone had better answer me. Susan? Michael?"

But before anyone could answer her, the bell rang. The class jumped up and dashed out the door like tiny comets.

No one looked at Katherine Ann.

The other person no one looked at was Jesse.

Rosey was waiting for Jesse after school. "You ouldn't have done it. Everyone is furious and not even supposed to *talk* to you. You'll have the consequences of your actions."

 are the consequences?" murmured Jesse.

d Katherine Ann—you're Living Dead

"But Rosey—"

"I tried to talk them out of it."

"But Katherine Ann *wants* to be friendly, she really does."

"Not allowed to say another word." And Rosey's eyes went blank, like she was mentally erasing Jesse. Then she headed off down the street alone.

14

The next day when everyone had to team up for art projects, no one picked Jesse. And when Elsbeth lost her pen and Jesse found it, Elsbeth refused to take it from Jesse's hand. Elsbeth acted like she didn't even see or hear Jesse. Jesse finally just laid it on Elsbeth's desk.

Katherine Ann was being absolutely quiet. Since her arrival at La Verne Elementary, this was the first day you could hear the sound of many voices answering questions. Jesse looked over at Katherine Ann. Who would have thought they'd ever be in the same boat—and sinking fast?

fter school most of the class disappeared in
d time. Katherine Ann had been the first to
But Tucker stayed behind to talk to Jesse.
's everyone cooking up against Katherine
sked.

"It's already cooked," said Jesse. "They . . . we . . . were trying to teach Katherine Ann a lesson. She was getting on everyone's nerves. Katherine Ann always has to know every answer and show off to impress everyone."

"So you were in on it too?"

"Yes. But then I broke the rules and I spoke to her, and now they're mad at me."

"She doesn't have to impress me," said Tucker. "I think she really understands the principles of solar energy."

"And everything else. . . ."

"You should be nice to her Jesse," said Tucker. "She's new."

"I should also be the first woman on the moon," said Jesse. "Anyway, I *am* nice to her."

What Jesse didn't say was how confused she felt.

"What's the matter?" The Hooter could always tell when Jesse was in the dumps.

"Nothing."

"You look awful."

"Thanks."

"Well, maybe not awful. Maybe dreadful. Apprehensive, ruined, horrible, ghastly."

"How about ghostly?"

"Sure. Ghostly. Why?"

"It's because I'm trying to live through the Living Death at school."

"What's that?"

"That's when everyone pretends you've passed on into the next dimension, even though you're in *this* dimension and standing there passing out their book reports."

"What did you *do*?"

"I talked to Katherine Ann when we had a plan not to."

"You did? You're the best, Jesse!" The Hooter ran and threw his arms around his sister. "And I bet your dance is going to be the best thing at 'We Are Wonderful Day.'"

"No way, Hooter. I haven't even learned all the steps yet."

"Why not?"

"I'm not sure. But I have my third lesson coming up in half an hour."

"Now, last time you were having trouble with the heel toe, heel toe, turn." Mrs. Franklin didn't waste a minute. "Here we go!"

Jesse tried to imitate her.

"No, dear, that turn has to be fast. Speedy, with punch. Like this." Mrs. Franklin threw her head back. "You still don't have a feel for the joy, the drama, of this dance. Try it again."

Jesse tried it again.

"No, no. Stomp, stomp, then turn!" yelled Mrs. Franklin.

Somehow, Jesse got the feeling that Mrs. Franklin wasn't in a dancing mood. Maybe she was tired of teaching Jesse. And tired of Jesse not getting anything right. Jesse concentrated harder.

"Stop! It's stomp, stomp, *point*! Arms up, smile! Oh, how will we ever get you in shape, Jesse? Have you done any dancing before this?"

"No, but my gym teacher said I was graceful."

"She did?"

Before they could discuss Jesse's gracefulness any further, Katherine Ann yelled from the kitchen, "The cookies are ready. You've got to try one!"

Mrs. Franklin turned to Jesse. "I guess we might as well. We're not getting very far, are we?" She flew over to the turntable and switched it off.

"Anyway," she said as she headed toward the kitchen, "I'm anxious to taste these. Katherine Ann invented the recipe."

"I didn't invent it, Mother," said Katherine Ann, holding warm coconut cookies on a tray. "I just followed the cookbook."

"But they taste so . . . special!" said Mrs. Franklin after biting a tiny edge of the cookie.

Jesse bit hers too. They were good.

"Well, Betty Crocker knows how to cook," said Katherine Ann.

"You added the almond, though, didn't you?" asked Mrs. Franklin.

"It called for almond."

"What about the coconut?"

"It called for coconut."

"You mean you simply followed the recipe?"

"Yes."

Mrs. Franklin looked as if she was having a hard time believing her ears. "But I told you to do something extra, to be creative."

"When I get too creative, like with my secret thing, you say I'm going overboard." Katherine Ann was getting all worked up. Jesse had never seen her like this before.

"There's nothing wrong with a little helpful criticism."

"Mom, I thought you would *like* these cookies."

"I do like them. I'm just trying to teach you that whatever you do, there's always an opportunity to outdo yourself."

"I'm tired of outdoing myself," said Katherine Ann. And she suddenly jumped up and ran out of the kitchen.

"You know, Jesse," said Mrs. Franklin, "when I was a girl, nobody pushed me. And I had many talents. That's why I push my daughter. For her own sake. Now let's push you a little, Miss Langston."

Jesse got up from the table slowly. "You've been very nice to try to teach me this dance," she said, "but I don't think I'm going to finish my lessons, Mrs. Franklin."

"Jesse! Don't be a quitter," said Mrs. Franklin. "That's not a healthy attitude."

"I want to thank you for helping me," said Jesse. "I don't know what I would have done without you trying to teach me the dance. But I think I'm just going to have to learn it on my own. OK?"

From the look on Mrs. Franklin's face it wasn't OK. But Jesse couldn't help that. She grabbed her jacket from the living room, zipped it up, and shouted to Katherine Ann, " 'Bye. See you in school." And then Jesse was out the door. The fresh air had never felt so good licking her cheeks, sliding up and down her coat sleeves, and blowing her hair.

She ran all the way home. It rained all weekend. And Jesse didn't try to dance even once.

15

"We have exciting news today," Mrs. Chakowski told her class on Monday. "The La Verne *Tribune* is doing an article about 'We Are Wonderful Day.' I want you all to make sure you'll be listed for the correct activity, so I'm going to pass the list around before I give it back to Rosey."

Everyone whispered as they passed around the piece of paper that would eventually go to the newspaper. But when Michael Peters handed it to Jesse, the whispering stopped. Michael didn't even look at her. It really was as if she had turned into a ghost.

Jesse wasn't sure if she should leave "Hat Dance" next to her name or not. Would she learn it in time? Jesse looked at Rosey. Rosey always had an answer.

But Rosey only turned away.

Then Margaret Prince was whispering—softly

enough so that Mrs. Chakowski couldn't hear, but loudly enough for everyone else to get the message: "Anyone who talks to Katherine Ann is in big trouble."

Jesse knew Rosey couldn't break the rules, or Rosey would be in the same fix as she was in. So Jesse left "Hat Dance" on the paper and passed it to the next aisle. Then she hardly looked up for the rest of the morning.

At lunch Rosey didn't sit down next to Jesse in their usual spot. In fact, their usual spot was completely empty. Rosey sat with Margaret and Susan. Jesse sat alone with her chicken pot pie. Then she heard Tucker and Katherine Ann putting their trays down at the table behind her.

"I'm glad you're using some of Jesse's design ideas," said Tucker. "I think Jesse is neat."

"Yeah, she is," said Katherine Ann. "But you know what, Tucker? Thanks to your doghouse I'm learning so many things I never knew about solar power. Maybe now I can get my dad to talk to me more."

"Your dad is a genius," said Tucker.

"I know," Katherine Ann said almost in a whisper.

Then they both sat down and started to eat lunch.

After school Jesse went home and put on her Mexican record. It was wonderful that Tucker still liked her; that made her feel tingly and good. And the music was so fast and happy that for the first time Jesse really felt like dancing. She remembered all the instructions Katherine Ann and her mother had given her. How to tap, tap, tap, then point, twist, snap, and bend. But her feet still refused to listen to her brain. Finally Jesse decided she would do her *own* steps. Nobody was there to watch her, and the music made her want to move.

Jesse danced just the way her body told her to. When she wanted to leap, she leaped. Jesse knew Mrs. Franklin was right about one thing: If you couldn't feel the joy, there was no reason to dance. For too long, learning these steps had been like schoolwork—something she *had* to do. But that wasn't what dancing was about. Dancing was about moving, and feeling the rhythms, and feeling free. Jesse twirled and stomped. Little bits of steps she had been taught would crop up here and there, and seemed to fit in perfectly. Jesse was feeling better and better. She was dancing and alive, and not feeling any of the effects of the Living Death. Phooey to everybody! They couldn't wipe her out.

Finally the song was over. Jesse was breathing hard and sweating all over as she went over to the record player to turn it off.

Then she heard applause. She turned toward the hallway. The Hooter and Katherine Ann were both clapping. They had huge grins on their faces.

"Excellent!" said Katherine Ann.

"Inspired!" said the Hooter.

"I agree. Jesse, I didn't know you could dance like that."

"Nobody was supposed to be here," said Jesse.

"Well, we didn't want to interrupt," said Katherine Ann. "You've learned it almost as fast as I did."

"Thanks."

"Well, that's why I came over. To see if you wanted help."

"Thanks again. But I think I'll just stick to it myself."

"OK," said Katherine Ann. "Then I guess I'll leave."

"Don't leave!" said the Hooter. "You're both part of the Living Dead, right? You two should be friends."

Jesse wished her kid brother would disappear.

"Anyway, what's your wonderful thing, Katherine Ann?" he asked quickly.

"I do lots of wonderful things, Hooter."

"But what's your favorite?"

"Well, I'm really enjoying working on the solar-powered doghouse."

"Is that your *very* favorite?"

"Hooter, don't pester Katherine Ann with questions," said Jesse. "It's not polite."

"I don't mind," said Katherine Ann. "Your brother is cute. I wish I had a brother."

"Thanks," said the Hooter. "So what's your very favorite thing, Katherine Ann? Is it solar power?"

"Well, I like solar power because my father is a solar engineer," said Katherine Ann. "Except I hardly get to talk to him. He's too busy. So I decided to get interested in what he does. Then maybe he'll find time to talk to me."

"Doesn't he take you with him when he goes to all those different countries?" asked the Hooter.

"He used to. But now he's traveling on top-secret business."

Jesse wished she could think of a way to stop Hooter from interrogating Katherine Ann. But secretly Jesse wanted to find out more about this mysterious family too.

"Do you miss your father?"

"Yes," said Katherine Ann. "Of course." Then for a minute Katherine Ann's one blue eye and one brown eye thoughtfully looked at Jesse, then back at Hooter, then back at Jesse again. "Know what?" she said slowly. "Maybe I will tell you what my favorite thing is. But it's my secret, so you can't tell. There is something I do, and it *is* wonderful."

"Then why's it a secret?" asked the Hooter.

" 'Cause my mother won't let me do it."

"Why not?" asked Jesse.

"She thinks it's low class."

"Well, what *is* it?" asked the Hooter, close to bursting.

"I play the saxophone." Suddenly Katherine Ann was smiling. "In my garage. It's an alto sax. My dad used to play it."

"Wow! What kind of music do you play?" asked the Hooter.

"I like rock and roll," said Katherine Ann. "I play lots of loud notes, and sometimes I have to breathe so hard I get dizzy. I like wailing on the sax more than pottery, or baking bread, or poetry."

"That's some great secret!" said the Hooter. "And it's not low class."

"Well, you and Jesse are the only ones on the whole North American continent to know. Promise you won't tell?"

"We promise," said the Hooter.

"Promise, Jesse?"

"Sure." Of course she wouldn't tell. Nobody was talking to her anyway. Who would she tell? A wall?

16

"She's beautiful," sighed the Hooter when Katherine Ann left.

"I know!"

"Then why can't she be your best friend?"

"Because *Rosey* is my best friend. And Rosey doesn't say things like 'you learned it almost as fast as I did.' "

"Well, what kind of best friend won't even talk to you?" Jesse's brother had his hands crossed in front of him like a tired policeman.

"She'll talk to me."

"When?"

"Someday."

"Someday! Don't you miss her *now*? Don't you want to talk to her right this very minute?"

"I suppose," said Jesse. "Sure, I wish I could call and tell her about my dancing. And how you fell head over heels for Katherine Ann."

"Some best friend," said the Hooter. "If you

called her up, she wouldn't even speak to you!"

"I don't know! *I* could talk to *her*, only I don't know if *she'd* talk to *me*."

"If she's your friend, your real true friend, she'd answer you. Otherwise, maybe you and Katherine Ann could become best friends. Then she'd come over almost every day."

"No chance," said Jesse. "Forget it."

A slightly disgusted Hooter headed into the kitchen.

Jesse thought about what he had said. Maybe he was right. In fact, maybe Rosey was sitting in her room wishing she could dial Jesse this very minute! Maybe she wished she could tell Jesse about playing Harold at chess, or complain how Margaret Prince never stopped talking. What if Rosey was feeling exactly like Jesse? Jesse took a deep breath and picked up the phone. Her heart was beating like it did when the alarm went off in school for a fire drill—loud and fast. Then she put the phone back down.

"Hooter," she yelled, "I can't take any more rejection. Want to go to the park?"

"Sure. Let me just get an apple."

Jesse and Hooter were on the swings when Jesse heard, "*Pssst*. It's me!"

Rosey was half hiding behind a tree.

"This is wrong, but I can't help myself. How are you doing, Jess?"

"OK. I quit my lessons with Mrs. Franklin. Then Katherine Ann came over to help me, she really tried to help, but I decided to do it by myself."

"She didn't say how she was a million times better?"

"Not exactly," said Jesse. "I don't think she can help herself from saying things half the time. Oh, and the Hooter fell in love with her."

"What does the Hooter know?"

"Well, one thing I know is her secret," said the Hooter.

"Secret? Oh, right! Well, what is it?"

"You know what she said? That she wished she had a brother. Probably one just like me."

"Is *that* the secret?"

"No, of course not," moaned Jesse.

"Well, tell me!"

"I *can't*! I promised. How's Harold?" Jesse hoped this would stop Rosey from asking her about Katherine Ann's secret.

"We're tied. He's won once, and so have I. I've got to go, Jesse."

"Why?"

"Because I'm violating the Living Death. But if you tell me the secret, then it will be for a worthwhile reason."

"Rosey, I'll just say one thing. I bet if Katherine Ann could *do* her secret, she'd be easier to be around."

"Really? How about if I guess? Then you won't be breaking a promise. Is it something about another country?"

Jesse didn't answer. But the Hooter piped up, "No."

"Is it a sport?"

"No."

"Is it speaking a language?"

"No."

"Is it some kind of performance?"

"You got it!" blurted the Hooter.

"*All right!* Thanks, pal. It's a . . . dance?"

"Nope."

"Oh *no*. She's an actress?"

"No."

"Then it's music. Something about music?"

Jesse tried not to let her face give it away.

"She plays an instrument," said the Hooter. Then he clapped his hand over his mouth. "I forgot I was only going to answer yes or no."

"Is it the drums? That's what I'd play."

"Nope."

"Of course not. Drums are not refined enough. Maybe it's the violin?"

"No. It's not classical music."

"The banjo? Harmonica? Guitar?"

"It's not country either."

"Don't tell me it's rock and roll."

Jesse's brown eyes rolled upward. She bit her lip.

"I'm getting closer, I can tell," said Rosey. "What could it be? Not the tambourine, you can't solo on it. Not the bass, it's too subtle. The flute maybe."

"No," said the Hooter. "It's much better."

"Better?" said Rosey.

"Well, louder," said the Hooter.

"Wait a second." Rosey's eyes glazed and half closed. "The loudest thing I can think of is the sax. Does that girl play the saxophone?"

"I'm not saying a word," said Jesse.

"But if she said a word," said the Hooter, "it would be alto sax. Her dad used to play it, but her mother thinks it's too low class."

"Don't tell Margaret," said Jesse. "She'll tell everybody, and then Katherine Ann will be furious with me."

"I totally promise I won't tell Margaret," said Rosey. "Margaret can be a real pain."

Then Rosey ran out of the park, making sure nobody from school was anywhere around. Just before the street she yelled, "Thanks, Hooter."

"Hooter, why'd you tell?" asked Jesse.

"I figured if Rosey knew, she'd like Katherine Ann more. And if Rosey liked her, then everybody'd like her. Then everyone's troubles would be over."

"You better hope Rosey can keep it classified information," said Jesse. "For both our sakes."

The next day Jesse could tell that everyone really wanted to be friends with her again. They had had it with the Living Death.

Jesse was called to the board to solve a math problem with Michael Peters. Jesse figured out hers, but Michael was standing there sighing, looking around, and fidgeting. In the good old days Jesse would have helped him, but now she pretended not to notice. The Living Death could work both ways.

After math Mrs. Chakowski announced a special visitor. It was Jacqueline Lawler from the La Verne *Tribune*. She had very short brown hair, and large eyes, and sort of stumpy legs. She was wearing a purple suit. Miss Lawler told the class she would be coming Wednesday to "We Are Wonderful Day," and would write it up for the paper. But today she was here so the class could ask her questions about journalism.

114

"Are journalists always honest?" Rosey asked.

"We try to be. We try to quote people correctly, but sometimes a piece can be distorted because it's shortened. Then the meanings can change."

"Is there a special science editor?" Tucker asked.

"At a large paper there is. But at the *Tribune*, which is small, we all cover science."

"Why do you like being a journalist?" Harold asked.

"Because it is full of surprises," said Miss Lawler. "And I travel, and meet people I'd never get to know otherwise. Like you."

After a few more questions Mrs. Chakowski told the class Miss Lawler had to leave to meet a deadline, but first would Rosey please give Miss Lawler the official class list for "We Are Wonderful Day" so she would be prepared to write the article.

Rosey was busy erasing and writing something, but she hurried up to finish. Then she marched up to the front of the room and handed over the list as if it was the most important document in history, another Declaration of Independence or the Constitution.

Miss Lawler took the list and said she would see everyone again, and left.

The class was excited about meeting the journalist who would be writing about them. Jesse looked around and wished she could buzz about it like everyone else, but she knew no one would talk to her.

Katherine Ann was calmly bent over a music book that she had been reading for days. She certainly didn't let the Living Death get to her. That girl was as strong as a horse.

But what surprised Jesse was that Rosey was also just quietly sitting in her seat. Even when Margaret came over to whisper to her, Rosey didn't seem to hear. And that wasn't at all like Rosey.

17

At home when Jesse put on her Mexican record, she hoped she'd feel the same sense of freedom she'd felt the previous night. She was trying to learn the end of the dance. But tonight nothing seemed to click.

There was a knock on the door. "Want to take a run?" her father asked. "Keep me company— I'm going over to the park."

"Sure!" Maybe if she got warmed up, the dance would come easier. Jesse put on shorts and a headband and ran out the front door, where her dad was jogging in place. He was in green sweats, which made his beard look almost orange.

Jesse tried her best to keep up with her dad, and she knew he was running extra slowly.

"How's the Hat Dance going?" he asked as they got to the park. "I'm glad the big night is on Thursday. Thursday is good for me."

"How'd you know it was on Thursday? Did you remember?"

"I read about it in the La Verne *Tribune*."

"It was in the paper already?"

"Sure. Tonight's late edition. 'We Are Wonderful Day' was announced with everyone's name, and what they're going to do. I was very proud to see your name in the paper."

"Thanks, Dad."

"I bet you're good by now. Better than good."

"I'm trying. But Dad, would you like me even if I wasn't good? What if I was just mediocre?"

Jesse's dad slowed down to a stop. He looked his daughter right in the eyes. "I love you, sweetheart. And that has nothing to do with how you dance, or do anything else. I wouldn't care if you moved like a sick elephant. Got it?" Then he swooped down and gave Jesse a big hug. She let herself melt into her father's big, sweaty arms.

Jesse let her dad take off ahead of her and sat down on a bench to think. She was lucky. Not like Katherine Ann, who had to be outstanding for her mother. All the time.

When Jesse got home, she grabbed the newspaper and found the article: "A Special Day at La Verne Elementary, by Jacqueline Lawler."

Jesse read the first paragraph, which told about her school and what "We Are Wonderful Day" was. That was followed by a list of the members of the class and what they would be doing. Suddenly her brown eyes froze. Next to the name Katherine Ann Millicent Franklin was printed:

"Rock and roll sax solo."

Rosey must have flipped her lid! How could she?

She dialed Rosey's number. "What got into you?" she asked. "You of all people! You *never* lie!"

"I didn't *lie*!" said Rosey. "What I did was the ultimate in truth."

"*What* are you *talking* about? You changed what Katherine Ann said she would do on 'We Are Wonderful Day.' "

"I changed it to what in her heart of hearts she wants to do most of all. Even you said she'd be happier and easier to get along with if she did it, Jesse!"

"She's going to kill me. What made you do it?"

"I had a hunch. And I still have it."

"Your hunch is going to turn our class topsy-turvy."

"My hunches are usually pretty good," Rosey said calmly.

"I hope you're right."

"Well, we'll find out tomorrow. At least tomorrow you'll be back among the living."

"Except when this news gets around, I might

119

wish I never left the Living Dead," said Jesse.

"Hey!" the Hooter shouted as he ran into the living room. "Katherine Ann's secret is in the paper? How did that happen?"

"I have to hang up," Jesse told Rosey. "See you in school."

She turned to the Hooter, who was eating a banana.

"You shouldn't have told Rosey. Rosey told the paper. It's a mess," said Jesse. "And I'm right smack in the middle of it."

"I guess we goofed," said the Hooter. "I mean, I guess . . . I . . . goofed, didn't I?" He stopped eating and looked at his sister. "Yep, I did."

"I do not understand," said Mrs. Chakowski. It was Wednesday morning, and she had the La Verne *Tribune* in her hand. "I just read the paper and saw that Katherine Ann is listed as playing the sax. Rosey, you gave our list to Miss Lawler. What's going on?"

Mrs. Chakowski couldn't ask Katherine Ann. There was no sign of her this morning.

"Rosey?"

"Well, I happened to have a piece of information that Katherine Ann wanted to play her sax for us more than anything," said Rosey. "And since everyone else is doing what they really want to do, I thought I would put down what Katherine Ann really wanted to do as well. So I changed the list."

"Rosey Roth, you've taken an extreme liberty that has had certain effects." Mrs. Chakowski took a letter from her desk, read it to herself, and put it back. "Class, you might like to know that we've been informed Katherine Ann is to be registered at the Britannia Academy because La Verne Elementary doesn't fit her needs. In other words . . ."

". . . Katherine Ann is history," said Margaret.

"She has *withdrawn* from this class. Can you imagine how that makes *me* feel?" Mrs. Chakowski's eyes were beginning to tear, and her blue eye shadow was getting runny.

Rosey shrugged. "I was only trying to help, Mrs. Chakowski. I'm sorry. But in the end you still may be surprised."

"This *is* the end," said Margaret. "Now we're all in big trouble, Roth. Because of you."

"All I can say," said Mrs. Chakowski, "is that I hope you all can figure out a way to keep the 'wonderful' in 'We Are Wonderful Day.' "

The line during lunchtime was more like a crazy squiggle. Everyone huddled together and wanted

121

to know *how* Rosey had found out the secret. The Living Death was over now, and the class would never even have a chance to find out if it had worked. Katherine Ann was gone for good.

"I didn't think she'd be pulled out of school," Rosey admitted. "We'll just have to think of a way to get her back."

"I don't know about you, Roth," said Margaret Prince, "but it's Tuesday and we only have until Thursday, so someone better think pretty fast."

Harold got out a pencil and notebook. "I'll take suggestions," he said.

"It's going to take true brilliance to come up with the answer to *this* one," said Elsbeth. "We need a genius."

"Well, I'll *try*!" said Margaret Prince.

That caused the only laugh of the day.

18

Jesse and Rosey walked toward Rosey's house, hardly saying a word. At last Jesse was back with her best friend, the one person she loved to talk to, and now there was nothing between them but a big empty silence.

Then they passed the enormous Franklin house. Suddenly Jesse grabbed Rosey's arm. "Let's go in."

"Are you kidding? They don't want to see us!"

"That's why we've got to go in. To explain."

"Go without me."

"No, Rosey. You caused all this trouble and you're coming with me."

Jesse knocked on the big front door. It slowly swayed halfway open.

"Hello!" she called. Then she stepped into the foyer. "Hello." But nobody answered.

"They're probably not home. Let's go," said Rosey.

Just then they heard voices coming from the dining room. Jesse didn't know why, but she walked closer to the sounds. Rosey followed.

"I don't *want* to go there!" they heard Katherine Ann shout. "Those kids at Britannia are little creeps! All they talk about is where they've traveled, what they're going to buy, or who their parents know. Today was a nightmare."

"Let's get out of here," said Jesse.

Rosey wasn't budging. "Are you kidding? This is good! She's describing herself."

"Katherine Ann, I want you to be exposed to the best, and the children at La Verne Elementary could hardly be the best. They encouraged you to play the saxophone."

"They *didn't* encourage me. They didn't even *know* about it."

"Someone must have known, Katherine Ann, for it to be in the newspaper."

"Mother, the Britannia kids are brats. Do you want me to turn into a brat?"

"You mean she has more to go to turn into a card-carrying brat?" whispered Rosey.

"We're spying!" Jesse whispered back furiously. "Come on!"

"I'm sure they aren't brats, Katherine Ann. They probably excel at many things. I wish I had had a chance to go to a school like that."

"Then *you* go there!" said Katherine Ann. "I already excel at lots of things. Except one. Having friends."

"Katherine Ann, you've had many advantages that make you a very special little girl. Maybe they didn't understand that at your old school."

"They *do* understand," moaned Katherine Ann. "That's why they don't like me."

"Well, then, that's their loss. You can't sink to their level."

"I don't believe this," said Rosey.

Jesse jabbed her friend with her elbow. "Let's go!" But Rosey wouldn't move.

"But mother," said Katherine Ann, "the thing is, it feels much more like *my* loss. I *like* the kids at La Verne Elementary. They're normal—and nice." Her voice was getting shaky. "And if I go to Britannia, I'll turn out to be such a spoiled . . . twerp, and nobody normal or nice will ever like me."

To Rosey and Jesse's surprise, Katherine Ann actually began to cry.

Jesse turned and tiptoed out the front hall of the house. Rosey followed behind. When they got outside, they ran all the way to Rosey's house.

"*Now* what?" Jesse asked when they were in Rosey's living room.

"Now we have a rescue mission. But at least

we know that our target wants to be rescued. That will help."

"How do we rescue her?"

"That's a good question," said Rosey. "A very good question. Shhhh. I have to think." Rosey lay down on the carpet and focused her eyes across the room, and an empty, cloudy look came over her face. "I've started."

"I should hope so," said Jesse as she shut the front door and headed home.

"What's the problem?" the Hooter asked when Jesse walked into the kitchen. He was busy picking raisins out of a carrot salad his mother had made, and putting them on a plate. "Is it the Hat Dance?"

"No. I've been practicing every night."

"Then it must be Tucker. Did you fall out of love?"

"I wasn't *in* love," said Jesse.

"It's the Living Death. It got to you."

"No. It happens to be about your dream girl, Katherine Ann. We have to figure out a way to get her back into school."

"She wasn't in school?" said the Hooter in a tiny voice.

"No. Mrs. Franklin read in the La Verne *Trib-*

une that Katherine Ann was going to play the rock and roll sax, and decided we were a bad influence. So thanks to your blabbing she's gone, and we're all in trouble unless Rosey can think of something."

"Has anyone asked Katherine Ann to come back?"

"Hooter, don't be simpleminded."

"Why not?"

"Rosey hates obvious tactics."

"But Katherine Ann might not."

"Yes, but . . ."

"Got anything better in mind?"

Jesse dialed Rosey. Hooter stood right next to her. He was grinning from ear to ear.

"Well, it's certainly not the kind of idea that gets your blood going," said Rosey, "but the situation is too tense to ignore any positive approach. OK. Tomorrow. After school. I'll call Tucker and Margaret." Rosey hung up.

"Just one thing, Jesse," said the Hooter. "I get to come too."

19

"Why did you bring the Hooter along?" said Rosey as they walked over to Katherine Ann's.

"He thought of it. And besides, Katherine Ann likes him."

"She's crazy about me," said the Hooter, eavesdropping as usual.

"Anyway, Rosey, you brought Harold."

"I didn't bring Harold. Harold brought Harold."

Rosey, Tucker, Harold, Margaret, the Hooter, and Jesse arrived at the Franklins' front door. Rosey knocked.

"Hello," she said in her most formal tone when Mrs. Franklin answered the door. "We'd like to visit with Katherine Ann."

"Come in, children. She'll be back any second." Mrs. Franklin was wearing a purple kimono with birds and flowers stitched all over it.

"Where is she?" asked Harold.

"She's being fitted for the Britannia blazer," answered Mrs. Franklin. "Meanwhile, would you like some banana apple juice?"

"Thank you," said the Hooter. "Sounds good."

The six of them waited by the big bay window in the living room while Mrs. Franklin went into the kitchen.

"It's pretty exotic in here," said Harold, looking around.

"What's exotic mean?" asked the Hooter.

"I can't believe there's a word you don't know," said Jesse. "Look it up. You have your dictionary with you."

"I can't be bothered with my dictionary now. There's so much to look at in here." The Hooter picked up a finger piano from Africa and started to pluck it.

"Hooter!" Jesse grabbed it from him.

"It's all right, Jesse," said Mrs. Franklin, bringing in a tray of juice. "By the way, Katherine Ann didn't mention she was expecting visitors."

"We just decided to come over," said Rosey.

"We want her to come back to La Verne," said Margaret.

"That's very nice of you," said Mrs. Franklin. "But I think Katherine Ann will prefer Britannia."

"That's right." Katherine Ann stood at the door

wearing a navy blazer with a gold insignia on it. "Look at this neat jacket I get to wear." Katherine Ann turned around so everyone could admire it. Jesse couldn't believe Katherine Ann was acting like her old superior self.

"We're sorry about the Living Death," said Harold. "It was a stupid idea."

"I'm sorry I told your secret," said Rosey. "I was the leak."

"And *who* was the drip who started the leak, Rosey Roth?" Katherine Ann glared at Jesse.

"It wasn't Jesse!" piped up the Hooter. "It was me. I thought I was helping."

"We want you to come back," said Jesse. "We do."

"Hah! You'll miss me like you miss a math quiz, or a broken ankle. You only want me to come back because you probably feel guilty. It's not because you like me. Why don't you come out and admit it?"

"I like you," said Tucker.

"Me too," said Jesse and Harold together.

"Of course they like you," said Mrs. Franklin.

"Well, frankly," said Margaret, "I know none of us is perfect . . ."

"Amen." said Rosey.

". . . but when Katherine Ann thinks she has

to be better than everyone . . . I'm sorry to have to say this, Katherine Ann," said Margaret looking straight at the girl, "you can be a real pill."

"It's a good thing *you're* never like that, Margaret," said Rosey.

"I know," said Margaret.

"I guess her class just has to get used to someone as rare and *exotic* as Katherine Ann," said the Hooter.

"Thank you," said Mrs. Franklin.

"But when she has to show off and impress everyone with her specialness all the time, it gets people aggravated." Margaret was the only one who seemed brave enough to face Katherine Ann's mother.

"But Katherine Ann simply *is* special, and she *is* better at most things," said Mrs. Franklin.

"Always being the best is the worst way of winning friends," said Harold.

"I don't agree," said Katherine Ann's mother.

"But *you're* not in the fifth grade," said Katherine Ann. "You know what, Mother? I don't like baking! I hate it. I wish I could just eat cookies out of the bag like everyone else."

"You can't eat regular cookies?" asked Hooter. "Why not?"

"Because I don't believe in the easy way," said

Mrs. Franklin proudly. "Not for me, and not for my daughter."

"Mrs. Franklin, your daughter belongs with us." Jesse had never imagined she could be so bold.

"I'm afraid I don't see why," said Mrs. Franklin.

"Why don't you come to 'We Are Wonderful Day'?" said Rosey. "Then maybe you'll understand."

"I just may do that, Rosey," said Mrs. Franklin. "It's not that I'm a snob. I only want the best for my daughter." Then Mrs. Franklin left the room making muffled sounds in her throat.

"Is she crying?" asked Jesse.

"That's all right," said Katherine Ann. "She usually gets better after she cries."

"Are you OK?" Rosey asked.

"Better than OK. I feel like—you're all on my side. Like—we're all on the same side." Katherine Ann hesitated. "I've never felt that way before."

"Will you come to 'We Are Wonderful Day'?" Tucker wanted to know.

" 'We Are Wonderful Day'? I wouldn't miss it for anything."

"But will you *do* something too?" asked the Hooter.

"You bet. And it will knock your socks off."

20

Thursday night Rosey was running around the decorated auditorium like the Mad Hatter. A "We Are Wonderful Day" banner looped across the stage. "Harold isn't *here* yet!" she wailed. "What if he turns yellow and doesn't show?"

"I thought you'd be glad," said Jesse. "You hate boys, remember?"

Rosey shot Jesse a look. "Hate is an ugly word. I don't hate anyone. Anyway, I want to beat him at chess—in front of everybody. Oh, look! There's Katherine Ann!"

Katherine Ann walked in wearing a demure mint-green dress. She was carrying a flute. Mrs. Franklin was on one side of her, and on the other side was a tall man who stood so regally, Jesse supposed he must be the mayor. Or could he be Katherine Ann's father? Before Jesse could wonder any more, Mrs. Chakowski, wearing her new red dress, new shoes, and sprayed-down hair, walked up onstage.

"Everyone please take your places. We'd like to get started."

She took out a piece of paper and glanced down at it nervously. "The La Verne Elementary School is happy to welcome all the parents and friends of Room 203." She was shaking from head to toe, and her voice was climbing several octaves as she spoke into the microphone.

The auditorium was completely full. Jacqueline Lawler was sitting in the front row with a tape recorder and notebook.

"Each year we look forward to 'We Are Wonderful Day,' when we can celebrate what we can do, what we can share, in a world growing more complex and frightening every day." Mrs. Chakowski was reading from her notes as carefully as if she were the president giving a televised address. "The children have been planning this event for months. I know you will love our program, so without further ado, here's our first 'wonderful' person, Jerry Grinder."

Jerry Grinder ambled up to the stage, wearing an old-fashioned pleated shirt, a straw hat, and a very serious expression.

"What I will read today is from *Pudd'nhead Wilson*, by Mark Twain."

134

"Adam was but human—this explains it all.
He did not want the apple for the apple's
sake, he wanted it only because it was for-
bidden."

Jerry looked up to see if everyone understood.
Most people were smiling and waiting.

"The mistake was in not forbidding the ser-
pent; then he would have eaten the ser-
pent."

Jerry read with passion. Maybe he would be an
actor someday. As Jesse listened, the Hooter leafed
through his dictionary to look up all the words he
didn't know.

Jesse was trying to sit very still so she wouldn't
mess up her costume. She tried not to think of
the dance. Had she learned the steps, or would
she get up there and forget everything?

". . . so that's my favorite chapter," Jerry was
saying, "and I'd like to leave you with this thought:

"Let us endeavor to live so well, that when
we come to die, even the undertaker will
be sorry."

Jesse translated this to:

Let us endeavor to dance so well, that when
we stop, even Mrs. Franklin will be sorry.

The applause broke through Jesse's thoughts. Jerry smiled nervously and left the stage, hugging his book so tightly that if it had been a person it would have suffocated.

"Thank you, Jerry, that gives us a lot to think about." Mrs. Chakowski beamed. "And now, Rosey Roth and Harold Smert will show us some chess moves."

"He's not *here* yet," Rosey whispered to Jesse. "What should I do?"

"Play yourself, like you did last year."

"I'd rather play Harold." Rosey got out of her seat, swung her ponytail around, and walked up to the stage with determination. She was wearing a matching blue skirt and blouse. Jesse wondered how long the blouse would stay tucked neatly into her belt. Not very long, she bet.

"Hi," said Rosey, walking up to the special table Harold had built. It was tilted, so the audience could see all the moves. "This chessboard was built with two kinds of natural poplar. Harold Smert made it with his dad's help. Harold beveled the edges, which isn't easy."

Poor Rosey! She really wanted Harold to be there.

Suddenly Harold appeared at the back of the auditorium. He galloped past the audience and bolted up the steps to the stage.

"Sorry, Rosey," he whispered. Then he sat down to play.

Rosey grinned. "This is Harold Smert. He will play against me."

"I will open using a standard approach," said Harold. "I'll move my pawn."

"And I will respond to his move like this," explained Rosey, and she lifted one of her pawns and moved it forward.

As they played, Harold and Rosey told why they made each move. When they'd played for a few minutes, Mrs. Chakowski said they should move to the side of the stage, and during intermission people could come and ask them questions.

Next, Elsbeth Lee, usually very shy, walked over to the piano with quick, confident steps. She sat down and began to play and sing "The Sound of Music."

Jesse closed her eyes. Elsbeth's voice was high and clear and went up and down the scale like a wind chime. When she sang, Elsbeth wasn't shy anymore. She knew exactly what she was doing.

When the song was over, everyone clapped loudly. Clapping the loudest was Katherine Ann. She really seemed to mean it.

Mrs. Chakowski was shaking like a small earthquake. "That was terribly moving. Thank you, Elsbeth."

Elsbeth was radiant. She smiled and bowed to the audience, then with the same quick steps as before hurried off the stage.

"And now Tucker T. Cobbwebber will demonstrate and explain the world's first—we think—Solar-Powered Doghouse."

Tucker wheeled the doghouse onstage. "In about forty minutes," he began, "the sun delivers to the earth's surface as much energy as mankind uses in a year's time. The solar energy that falls on America in one *minute* is enough to supply the total energy needs of the *whole country* for one day! I think the doghouse is a good way to begin to harness the sun's energy."

Tucker explained how he had constructed his invention. Katherine Ann had done a big blueprintlike drawing, and pretty soon most of the audience seemed enthralled with what he was saying. Miss Lawler was scribbling furiously in her notebook.

"How did you get the idea?" someone in the audience asked.

"When Pfeiffer shed, my mother wouldn't allow him in the house. But it was cold in his doghouse, and he used to whine. I didn't want my mother to be upset, or my dog to be cold."

During the applause Tucker could have been

the sun, he was beaming so much light. Finally he wheeled the doghouse offstage, and the audience got quiet. Mrs. Langston gave Jesse a smile and a wink when Tucker left the stage.

"Oh . . . I . . . yes!" Mrs. Chakowski seemed to get more and more flustered with each student's success. "And now we have strawberry punch and intermission."

Jesse ran over to the chessboard. "Who's winning?"

"We're neck and neck," said Harold.

"Are you nervous?" asked Rosey.

"Petrified. Mrs. Franklin is here, and she'll know all my mistakes."

"At least Katherine Ann made it," said Rosey. "I wonder what's in store for us later."

21

When everyone was reseated after intermission, Mrs. Chakowski announced Susan Northral.

Susan looked unnerved. "I'm not next," she hissed to her teacher.

Mrs. Chakowski looked down at her list. "Yes you are, dear—come right up."

Susan looked even more flustered. "No *I'm not!*" she said. "I'm after Margaret."

Mrs. Chakowski looked back down again. "Oh . . . yes, oh dear, of course. Margaret?"

"Haya, haya, *haya!*" shrieked Margaret as she leaped onstage in full karate gear. She astonished the crowd with her wild jumps, her frenzied kicks, and her kamikaze turns.

"She's fierce," whispered the Hooter.

Margaret looked like she might explode any minute.

"She's like a human bomb," said Tucker.

Margaret was having so much fun up there, it seemed she might never want to get down off the stage. Mrs. Chakowski finally had to jump in and calm her down so she could announce Susan Northral and her loom demonstration.

After everyone learned about looms, Michael Peters got up and sang his song about the Loch Ness monster. That was when Jesse started to feel tingly and nervous, and had to try to breathe deeply. She was next! Everyone would be watching her. She wanted Tucker to think she was graceful and spunky, and she wanted her parents to be proud. Even though her dad said they loved her no matter what.

Finally Mrs. Chakowski announced her. Jesse got the hat and put it in the center of the stage. She put her feet in the starting position, and hoped she looked a little bit Mexican. Her hair was piled up, and she was wearing Extremely Red lipstick and large clip-on silver earrings. She looked down at her brightly colored skirt, and then looked out at the audience. All the people she knew were there, but it was Tucker's face that popped out at her. He was smiling. Jesse took one last deep breath and nodded to Mrs. Chakowski to turn on the record. The music began.

Jesse clicked her feet together, racing to keep

up with the beat. She snapped and twirled. She did all the steps and hardly worried because it was all happening so fast. Most of the time she landed just when the beat went *bam bam bam!*

Jesse remembered the night when the dance became her dance. She remembered the joy, and she let herself feel it again. Jesse flew around the hat like a crazy gypsy. No! Like a Mexican Hat Dancer. Two more twirls, a leap, and a stomp, stomp, stomp, and then the music finished. She was in her final position! Unbelievable! It was all over.

Now two huge grins dazzled her from the audience—her mother's and father's. There was even a grin on the Hooter's face. The audience was clapping and shouting, "Olé." Jesse stood there for a minute feeling how good it all was, and hoping she could remember this feeling for a long time. Finally, she walked offstage and sat down. A hand tapped her shoulder, and she turned around to see Tucker leaning over her.

"Know what, Jess? You're the best. The best dancer, the best girl."

"The best?" Jesse looked into Tucker's green eyes and saw that he meant it. "Glory," she muttered under her breath.

"What?" said Tucker.

"Thank you," said Jesse. Then she flashed Tucker her best, happiest smile.

"Whew!" sighed the Hooter. "I guess your crisis period is almost over."

Just then they heard Mrs. Chakowski announce that unfortunately there had been a misprint in the newspaper. Katherine Ann Franklin would be playing her flute, *not* the saxophone.

"The head of the Britannia Academy has requested Mozart, and in his honor, that is what I will play." Katherine Ann looked like a boiled-down vegetable in her green dress. It wasn't her best color.

So that tall man with Mrs. Franklin hadn't been Mr. Franklin! Katherine Ann must not have been exaggerating when she said she never saw her father. And if the head of the Britannia Academy was here, did that mean that she wasn't coming back to La Verne?

Suddenly from the side of the stage someone shouted, "Checkmate!" Rosey jumped up and grabbed Harold's hand.

Mrs. Chakowski didn't know which way to look. "Katherine Ann, would you mind waiting for just one minute? I believe our chess game is over."

Harold stepped up to the microphone. "I never thought she could take my king. But she did. Rosey

Roth may be this year's chess champion, but I want a rematch."

"You got it, Harold," said Rosey. "That was the most challenging game of chess I've ever played." Rosey pumped Harold's hand vigorously.

Jesse had never seen Harold smile before. His whole face changed. He took Rosey's hand and led her offstage like she was a queen.

When it was quiet again, Katherine Ann stepped up to the mike. "I will accompany a Boston Symphony recording with my flute." She lowered the needle onto the record, walked back to center stage, and began her piece. The notes were long and melodic, but a little sad. Mrs. Franklin whispered to the tall man. Then she began to smile as if Mozart himself were onstage. Katherine Ann went on playing the haunting melody.

Suddenly, there was an annoying scratch on the record. Completely unflustered, Katherine Ann stopped playing and walked over to the turn-table.

"There seems to be a problem," she said. She put down her flute and removed the record. Then she replaced it with another one. Katherine Ann sprinted offstage for a minute, and when she came back, she was carrying a saxophone!

"Hit it, boys!" she said as she started the record.

Suddenly a punk band began to bang out pulsing, blasting notes.

Katherine Ann ran back to center stage and started blowing into the big alto sax. She made loud squealing noises that sort of went along with the melody. Then she made the sax squawk. And when she stopped squawking, she honked. Jesse had never heard sounds like this before. It was like a traffic jam trying to sing a tune.

Katherine Ann jumped all over the stage making wild, jerky motions. Then she lowered her sax, and sang:

"You want to be wonderful,
You can't go it all alone.
To really be wonderful
You might run away,
Run away, you might run away from home."

The man from the Britannia Academy turned whiter than bleached underwear. He croaked something at Mrs. Franklin, then leaped up from his seat and headed for the exit. Mrs. Franklin ran after him. But at the back door she stopped, turned again, and looked at her daughter. She didn't seem to know what to do. Finally, with a dumbstruck look on her face, she went back to her seat and sat down.

By now the entire audience was clapping along to the beat. At some point Mrs. Franklin started to clap too.

Jesse sighed a big sigh of relief—until she looked at Mrs. Chakowski's face. It was purple.

Onstage, Katherine Ann tore the rubber band out of her hair, and ripped open her dress. Underneath was a pair of shiny shorts and a silver T-shirt. Now she looked like the punk rockers you saw on T.V.

> "*All alone,*
> *All alone,*
> *You can't go it all alone.*"

The record went on, and Katherine Ann got wilder and wilder. Rosey yelled, "Go, Katherine Ann, go!"

"All right!" Margaret Prince popped out of her seat and headed for the stage. She started kicking and doing her karate moves in time to the music.

"This is hot!" she yelled.

Meanwhile, Katherine Ann kept singing, or shouting, or whatever it was she was doing. Then she picked up her sax again and really made it scream. She acted as if some wild beast inside her had finally been let loose.

Elsbeth Lee was dancing onstage now. Harold

Smert joined her. Then Michael Peters ran up and Rosey followed next. Tucker grabbed Jesse's hand and they ran up together. The last person to go up was Susan Northral. She walked up quietly and stood at the back of the stage and swayed. Everyone from Room 203 was dancing onstage with Katherine Ann except Mrs. Chakowski. She was hiding behind her notes and looking appalled.

The La Verne *Tribune* photographer was taking pictures and caught it all.

Suddenly there was silence. The record was over. Katherine Ann walked over to the microphone and said, "So much for Mozart!"

The audience went wild. And the class knew that Katherine Ann was coming back to Room 203 for good.

Afterward Tucker led the *Tribune* photographer and Miss Lawler over to Rosey and Jesse. On the other side of him was Katherine Ann.

"These are the people who helped me," said Tucker. The photographer got ready to snap a picture.

"Well, Tucker," said Miss Lawler, "which one is your girlfriend?"

"That would be Jesse," said Katherine Ann.

"We're just friends," said Jesse while the pho-

tographer snapped a picture. The flash temporarily blinded them and nobody knew that Tucker bent over and gave Jesse a kiss on the cheek.

But the next day that was one of the shots—along with another of a horrified-looking Mrs. Chakowski watching everyone dancing with Katherine Ann—that appeared in the newspaper. So then everybody knew.

"Boys are trouble," said Jesse the next day on the telephone. "Much too much trouble. But there's something about them I like."

"Yuck!" said Rosey. "I don't like boys, and I never will."

"Never? What about Harold?"

"Well, Harold might be all right."

"But you don't like Tucker, right?"

"Come on, Jesse, you know I like Tucker most of the time."

"Oh, then it must be the Hooter who gets to you."

"That's ridiculous. I love the Hooter."

"I see," said Jesse. "You just don't like *boys*."

"*Right!*" said Rosey loudly.

Jesse covered her mouth to try to hold back her giggle. But she didn't have to because Rosey started to chuckle. They both laughed and laughed until they got off the phone.